WORKING FOR LOVE

WORKING FOR LOVE

TESSA DAHL

Delacorte Press

Published by
Delacorte Press
The Bantam Doubleday Dell Publishing Group, Inc.
666 Fifth Avenue
New York, New York 10103

Library of Congress Cataloging in Publication Data

Dahl, Tessa.
  Working for love.

  I. Title.
PR6054.A354W67   1989   823'.914   88-20348

ISBN 0-440-50114-8

Manufactured in the United States of America

February 1989

10 9 8 7 6 5 4 3 2 1

BG

To my father

PART
ONE

chapter
1

Dear Jack,

I was appalled when Carol told me of your telephone
conversation. You left me for my *own* good, I gather.
It was the only way that you felt I would get on with
my life.

How much more patronizing can you *become?* It
reminds me of the parental "this is hurting me more
than it will hurt you." Oh no, you've got it *wrong.* But
once again you've become the martyr. Once again the
great underminer is at work. And now I suppose if I
do get on with my life, if I do find some success, then
it's all thanks to you, for leaving me?

When we had dinner last week, I told you that this
was going to be *my* year. Nineteen eighty-seven and

I'm thirty in April. I'd tried self-destruction, I'd tried apologizing for my existence, I'd tried to be everyone but me and to please the whole male population headed by you and Daddy. *No longer* am I going to apologize for being alive—I'm going to get on with my life.

So I asked you for a little cooperation. I suggested that perhaps you could start treating me as your equal and less like a child? Stop sapping my confidence every time I start to become powerful? Stop questioning my moves and telling me what I'm thinking (especially when I'm not)? You replied that you had a deep-rooted conviction that I blame everyone for the way I am and feel. That really I just want to be treated like a child.

Thus we were totally incompatible, you said, because all the while I'm asking you not to undermine me, you know that I'm just blaming you for how I am anyway. You had me in a no-win clinch.

"What would you really like me to say?" I begged you. (Why do you always manage to make me beg?)

"I want you to say that irrespective of how I treat you, you're going to get on with your life."

"But that is what I'm saying. I am going to become successful. This is my year. But I would like you to try and stand beside me as an equal and stop gnawing at my foundations."

"I'm sorry Molly, I don't think I can promise to do that. I can't come to terms with your alleged search for fulfillment. Why can't you be satisfied to stand by me and help turn my company into a giant?"

Working for Love

Oh Jack, it's all there isn't it? You can't bear it when I glow. Every time a whiff of confidence gusts toward me you have to divert it. And now, now I want to start living my life, you tell me you can't be a partner to that.

And all the while you were telling me that you were leaving me "for my own good," you were stuffing yourself. Lobster and foie gras salad, steak au poivre and eventually, as the petits fours became petits sevens and eights, I said, "You're quite a chap, aren't you Jack? I thought I was getting a lovely surprise, going out to the restaurant we had our wedding reception at, but you sit there and scoff away and between mouthfuls tell me you want to separate. While I feel completely stunned, sickened."

"This isn't an eating competition Molly," you said.

On the way home you informed me that you would support me financially during this separation period, and that you hoped that I realized that this was the only answer.

Can't we work on this problem together Jack? I don't want to sit alone with the children in the country, on your payroll—I want to be your wife. Then you dropped me home and you left for London. Your headlights flashed over me as you turned the car. You could see me sobbing—bent over the wall— banging my fists.

You thought I wouldn't get through the first day without you. You thought I'd be on the phone screaming for you to come back. Not this time Jack. I don't care about the endless let's-make-fun-of-Molly stories you tell people so they can say "Poor Jack." I don't care that you haven't called me for two weeks now. I don't care that you're in London and I don't know what you're doing.

Oh, but I do care. I care so much I'm bursting. But this is a power game. I'm not going to lose this time. I've bent in every direction to make you happy. I've cried out and craved for your attention and approval, I've always thought that if I could make you happy, then we'd be safe. That if I pleased Daddy and now you, then I would be okay. That didn't work.

Guess what? I'm going to be okay on my own.

I love you Jack and if I sit and think of our marriage and what has happened, it hurts so much that I can hardly bear to breathe.

Would you like to read a story Jack? I'd like to tell it.

It's a story of a fight. A life that you've never known about. Where yours had total security, this one has none. For all the normality you had, this has abnormality. Where you were told relentlessly how brilliant you were, this person was not. Oh, but she was privileged. Whereas you had your middle class, stable home, she was surrounded by glowing, gifted people and things.

I'm sure you're bored of hearing stories about rich girls who blow their brains out on drugs and blame their parents for their lack of incentive. That's not what this is. I know how privileged I am. I blame no one for my extraordinary life. I thank them for it. It's made me what I am and my darling, I've decided I like it.

chapter

2

My parents were a glorious couple. My father was a giant. Every year or two he would become immersed in a new hobby. He would learn everything about it, spend a fortune on it, and then, once he had the answers and the novelty had worn off, he'd drop it. He was like that with people too. Everything he did he was to excel at. We were all in total awe of him.

Every morning at seven-thirty he would be ready to drive us to school; on the way there he'd sing times tables with us. He'd tell us stories and squeeze our personalities into shape. Filling us with spark and fascinating ideas. The love of his life was my older

sister, Mary. She always sat in the front and together
they would sing little songs.

Mary and Papa went in the car
What did they see in the fields afar?
They saw lots of baby pigs
Piggy wiggy wiggy wiggy wiggy wiggy wigs.

Then they would laugh with each other. Mary was
everything he wanted. Daddy and Mary would go off
and fiddle around. Making a little garden or wander-
ing off to the woods together to look for mushrooms.
Lifting stones in the garden and studying the ants'
nests underneath. It was their world and we didn't
share it with them. She was the only person he ever
openly loved.

Never would my father give an ounce of emotion.
His chest was tight. It was all stored in there and
never let out. But we knew he cared.

Physical contact was taboo and feelings were dismissed. We used to crawl into Mummy and Daddy's
bed in the night, and if, by chance, my leg touched
his or my arm brushed his side, he would kick out like
a horse and move as far away as possible. My mother
would entwine legs. She would cuddle in bed until
we gasped for air. She was a beautiful, loving, vital
woman. Every emotion she ever felt came tumbling
from her. Every hurt or success was echoed around
our house.

"Oh Papa," she used to say to Daddy, "do you love
me?"

"Don't ask such bloody stupid questions Rachel."

That was when our lives were perfect. Untouched. If someone had lifted the stone up to look at us, they would have seen our happiness. Oh, we were different and knew it. Our house was filled with beautiful seventeenth- and eighteenth-century furniture, bought cleverly at little country auctions by my father and lovingly restored (one of his past whims). We had remarkable paintings on the walls—he bought Francis Bacons when they were £2,000 each, and a little Matisse would be hung by a framed drawing by Mary or myself. Everywhere there was clutter, stylish clutter, all products of my parents' work. No inheritance for them.

My ravishing mother was born in a small town in Iowa; her parents ran a pet shop. Her ambition to be an actress strangled her working-class background. She aimed herself with terrifying determination and broke into Hollywood at twenty and became a film star. My father happened upon her eight years later in London, where she was on tour with a play. He thought she was beautiful and showed promise. He thought he could prize her away from America, teach her about antiques, art, and wine, and then perhaps he could overlook the actressy part of her. But he didn't know then, film stars never really change.

He needed her. She was a serious money-earner. He was an unknown artist. A hero from the Second World War, with no money. She was quite willing to marry him. Her life in Hollywood had become torrid

—an escape route was welcome and she wanted beautiful babies.

Two things happened for the first and last time on their wedding night. He told her he loved her, and he put on a nightshirt and never slept nude again.

They moved to a Georgian farmhouse in England. He painted in a studio she had built in the garden, while she went out and acted, earning a lot of money. They had Mary, then me, then my brother, Mathew, and it was all idyllic.

Suddenly the stone crashed down on our nest, as if someone was bored with the perfection of it. It crushed our lives forever and turned our existence into turmoil.

chapter
3

Incidentally Jack, just for the record, I don't need your patronizing, shit-eating company.

When you looked at me across your steak au poivre as I asked, "But what about our holiday Jack?" you narrowed your eyes and challenged, "Go on your own."

"Oh yeah, sure thing," I replied.

"No Molly, I mean it."

You never believed in a million years that I would or could. The holiday that we'd been planning for six months. The holiday of my dreams.

I called the travel agent the next morning and inquired, "Have you spoken to my husband?"

"Oh yes, twice last week."

"And is everything arranged?" I asked cautiously.

"Oh yes, he canceled the holiday on Tuesday."

I felt totally betrayed. You canceled our holiday before you told me you wanted to separate. Five days before.

That left me with two weeks free and a lot of anger. So I planned a holiday alone.

I would confront myself and my fears and go. I would prove to myself that I was capable on my own.

And you Jack, would be surprised, amazed, and gobsmacked when you discovered that I had gone.

I did it and here I am.

It's lonely but I'm free. I'm not explaining myself to anyone. I don't need you here to validate me. People actually talk to me. I was worried that they'd feel sorry for me and bound to talk. So I make a point of sitting alone on the beach and looking like I want to. Or walking away from a conversation before they do. All couples, and me.

Last night I cried. I suddenly realized that I was frightened of going to the bar in case no one wanted to talk to me. Then I thought that if you were here, I wouldn't be frightened and they'd talk to me so why shouldn't it be the same with just me? I went and it was lovely. Everyone chatted. We all laughed and I felt totally in command when I left my new friends early to go to bed.

But today it hit me Jack. You see, I have this churning that works on the same system as my new tumble dryer. For half a cycle the drum turns upside down and for the other half it turns the right way up. I

gather myself together and think how wonderful it is
to be on my own, how clever I am to be here. How
confident and exhilarated I am. Who needs Jack? I
think, I'll show him, and I have a gush of relief that
we are apart, knowing that it is a great thing to be
striking for self-respect. But then I look at the sugar
mill where we had our truly most idyllic holiday and I
ache. I hurt so deeply for what joy we had, what
promises we made each other. But you, you
controlling bastard, couldn't deal with it even then,
could you?

"I'm so happy Jack, can't you see how I thrive
when you're giving me time?" I'd ask.

"Don't be silly Molly, it's only because you think
you're pregnant."

I could count the number of times I've said to you,
"Oh please Jack, just take some notice of me and I'll
blossom. All I want is to be your own special person. I
only get nasty when I'm ignored."

You know, I didn't mind you working from five A.M.
to nine P.M. I didn't mind the fact that you loved your
work far more than me. I asked for your leftovers.
When you came home from work, to listen to me,
make me feel important, and understand me. Okay,
not understand, but accept.

Do you remember when I asked the vicar to give
the sermon on acceptance? Four years ago Jack? The
deep need in a relationship for accepting one another.
But you couldn't, could you? You couldn't accept my
emotional outbursts. My strong feelings that would
flare for a minute.

"Christ, I hate my sister."

And then later that day I loved her. You couldn't cope with that—nothing impetuous or irrational for Jack. Everything has to be analyzed.

If I had a silly whim, you wanted to know why. To dissect it and control it. Ah, but there was no data.

"Why are you doing that Molly?"

"For fun Jack."

"No you're not, you're doing it to impress Paul."

"I'm not, darling."

"Yes, you are."

You had to tell me why and how and what my every move was for. And the more I started to become independent, the more you'd sit me down and tell me exactly what I was really doing and why, and even what I was going to do next.

You were wrong. You were always wrong. Because, as you'll discover as you read on, you'll never know about a mind that's lived this life. Not your little insular, safe life where you slipped from your adoring mother to university to controlling your own company —but mine.

I asked you to love me Jack.

And last night the owner of the hotel, he moved me from my lovely little cottage where I was so cozy and secure, where I had felt I belonged even though I was alone, to a new unfinished room in the middle of nowhere. All the couples had refused to budge and the hotel was overbooked. I wanted to help. No one else would go in it.

But once I'd hung up my clothes, stared at the gray,

unfinished walls, I realized I was very alone. Way, away from the hotel. I started to cry. Really cry— something I hadn't allowed myself to do since you left. Then I wailed and sobbed and spoke and shouted.

"I'm so fucking alone, you bastard. Why do I have to be alone? Why me, down in this concrete cell? Why do you have to punish me for wanting to just be me?"

But I sorted myself out, alone. It didn't take long and I decided I am really angry with you. If you can't control, you don't want to play, do you?

Didn't your mother ever say, "Play the game others want to play sweetheart."

I got through it and I changed rooms today. I'm learning to be assertive. But I'm craving, I'm craving those days when you used to love me and remember to buy me something on our anniversary. When you used to hold me so tight and cry with joy when we made love. When I felt totally filled with love.

Do you remember about six weeks ago in bed, when I begged you to hold me as tight as tight? Sighing, you turned away.

"Why is it never enough Molly?"

chapter
4

I was standing beside the pram on the sidewalk in New York City. Our nanny was in a hurry. She'd just been to pick me up from school. My new baby brother was in the pram, the pride and joy, the third child and the only son.

The lights changed and Jenny darted over the road with me hanging on to her and she pushing the carriage.

Screeching-screaming brakes, screeching-screaming Jenny, a crack of a yellow taxicab hurtling into a blue baby carriage, a little boy being thrown across a throbbing New York street, slamming into a bus; and me, standing useless, watching, knowing. The ambulance came, siren wailing. The little baby Mathew was wrapped and we were all herded into the ambulance, speeding to the hospital. My mother heard the siren and knew, a stab, an icicle went through her: she ran home and rallied my father and together they rushed to Lenox Hill.

From then on all life was centered on this little pathetic boy. Blinded, brain-damaged, and unconscious.

Each person had the added suffering of their own guilt.

My mother felt it was entirely her fault. If she hadn't been an actress, then they wouldn't have been in New York. She always took her family to New York for the winter while she worked on Broadway. But she was getting double messages. One side of her knew that she had to work to earn the money for the family, but if she hadn't been working, we would all have been in England and Mathew would not have been injured. If she didn't work, then we wouldn't have had a nanny to push Mathew into the bus. And Daddy, who knew that if he wasn't set on becoming an artist, then Mummy wouldn't be in New York. And the nanny, her unhappiness was inconsolable. But my parents did a very odd thing, trying to relieve her guilt, they made her Mathew's godmother.

The little boy lay in hospital in New York for weeks. We, Mary and I, went pretty well unnoticed during that period. All of my parents' energies were centered on their little boy. Eventually my father decided that the best help for Mathew was in London at Great Ormond Street.

We packed up and headed home.

Daddy immersed himself in helping his son recover.

Mummy immersed herself in work.

At home the tension lessened. Mary and I started to get a little more time and attention.

I've read my baby book for that year—Mummy wrote:

Poor Molly was with Jenny and Mathew when he was hit and it was a terrible experience for her. She was taken to the hospital in the police car; she behaved wonderfully, and cleverly stayed on the sidewalk and didn't run into the street. She knew how serious it was and asked me if Mathew would ever come home again. She was nervous and frightened of many things, particularly crossing streets, she began wetting the bed which continued until we came to England. She is slowly getting over the ghastly experience. She is terribly intelligent, she has a magnetic, strong personality and is a devil with the men.

chapter
5

I'd been longing to call home Jack. Aching to hear
your reaction when you'd found out that I had gone
on holiday. I delayed calling all day and built up the
anticipation.

Eventually I dialed. Helen, my mother's help,
answered the phone.

"Have you told him I've gone yet?"

"Yes."

"What did he say?"

"He said 'Well done Molly.' "

"And that's all?"

"I'm afraid so."

"He didn't even ask if I'd gone alone?"

"No, he didn't."

Why don't I learn? I mean, why don't I learn? Of course you're not going to show any outward surprise or emotion or even interest. You wouldn't give me that pleasure, would you? Why do you always catch me out?

Okay, hang on. I'm not going to allow this to bury me. Why did I go on this holiday? To surprise you or to surprise me? To give myself pleasure or to freak you out? Stop, count, and think. You're not going to manage to blow my mind from a million miles. Your little patronizing reaction might sway me, your total lack of interest stun me.

But why aren't you interested Jack? Couldn't you care just a little?

You see, I'm so in control, I'm dealing so well with this situation and you hate it.

You liked me best two months ago, unconscious, didn't you darling? I thought you were being so sweet, but now I understand. Dr. Roberts decided he had to operate. You came from your office just as I was climbing onto the trolley to take me to the operating room.

Why Dr. Roberts asked you if you'd like to watch the operation, I don't know. He could have asked me if I minded. Just as the anesthetist had pumped the anesthetic into my hand, Dr. Roberts came in and announced that you were going to watch.

"I don't think that's a very . . ."

Clunk, I was out.

The next thing I knew was you were by my bedside.

WORKING FOR LOVE

"Did you really watch darling?" I asked.

Oh God Jack, I kept coming around from the anesthetic and gazing at you sitting there and thinking how wonderful you were for being with me and telling you how much I loved you.

But then, as I got better, it started to dawn on me. As you would describe the operation to people. "The cutting, the stabbing," you said, with gory satisfaction.

The oddest thing of all, the revelation three weeks later of how the student nurse had forgotten to tighten the stirrup and how my leg had crashed to the floor like "dead meat."

And even though I'd complained of a sore leg prior to your revelation, you said how silly I was—how could I have a sore leg when it was my womb and tubes that were having surgery? No one went near my leg, you said. And the D & C Jack, you watched them put a knife up my cunt and gouge me out.

You liked me best unconscious, didn't you.

And I loved the attention—for a whole afternoon you were with me.

chapter

Just as the family were re-
covering. Just as my parents stopped having to rush
to and from Great Ormond Street with Mathew.
When our lives were returning to normality. Once
again we went to school, with Daddy and Mary sing-
ing; we would sit in the garden at six or seven o'clock,
chatting as the English summer gently unwound us;
we would make hot air balloons with Daddy and send
them into the sky; we would race to the fire station
and follow the fire engine when we heard the siren,
and I remember we woke up one morning to see our
names written out on the grass. The fairies had done

it, Daddy told us. He had sneaked out and drawn it with weed killer at midnight.

Oh, joyful life. Oh, how I can still feel the perfection of that English summer. Mummy would go to London at night to do a play and Daddy would take us on "spooky walks" up to the "witches' tree" and there he would tell us stories. We tingled and glowed and I, I was happy to take second place, for I had never known any other. Mary held the key and I sneaked in behind her. She won the high jump at school that summer and the celebrations at home were enormous. I was honored to be her sister. I, who could genuinely not step over a pile of books without sending them toppling to the floor, I can honestly say that I never felt any jealousy or resentment toward my glorious older sister, because it was simply accepted that she was special. We had a joint birthday party, my sixth and her seventh.

The photographs are in the album, I look at them often. She was beautiful and willowy, translucent and glowing. I was rather sweet and chubby.

A couple of days after our party, Mary got the measles. I went to Paul Haver's birthday party and I was given a little Indian doll as my going-home present. I gave it to Mary, because I truly loved her and I was so sorry that she hadn't been able to go. Later that evening, when my aunt came to see Mary, my mother led my aunt upstairs. From that moment our lives changed forever. As the two women walked up the stairs and into Mary's room, they toppled unwittingly over the edge of a jagged cliff-face into a canyon of darkness which was filled with such sadness, such total devastation that we would never recover.

chapter

7

The book I am reading has a chapter on giving your children high self-esteem Jack.

It says:

You must not ignore them, lecture them, order them, control them, demand obedience from them, reject them, put them down, withdraw from them, or dominate them. Rather than leading to high self-esteem, these behaviors lead to anger, frustration, anxiety, withdrawal, self-doubt, fear, insecurity, defiance, rebellion, self-hate, alienation, resentment, dependency, hostility, submission, compliance, and failure.

I read it and laughed out loud. That's us Jack, isn't it? Not us and our children, I mean you and me. How can you say that the way you treat me should not reflect in my behavior? How could you say that I blame you for the way I am naturally? I'm not taking that shit anymore. For seven years I dealt with all the nouns in that first sentence and it does lead to all the nouns in the second. So why are you feeling sorry for yourself? Why are you angry with me? Can you truly say that I am completely to blame—that you are blameless?

Did your first wife have a nervous breakdown, did she have affairs because you were such a good egg? Sorry, that's out of bounds. Tasteless, taboo.

Listen to me Jack. I loved you, I loved you so much I thought I could never love like it. Relentlessly, through seven years, I, puppy-like, went on accepting that I was a wastrel, a leech on your money and energy, and you went on believing it. From the minute you got up at 4:45 A.M. (no one said you had to be the first in your office) to the second you fell asleep for the final time, you despised me. You harbored a bitterness toward me that expanded over the years. I wasn't like the others you had known, was I? But Jack, that was what first attracted you to me, wasn't it? Your mother devoted herself to your father and promised him on his deathbed that she wouldn't marry again. She was always there for him and you. When we married she gave me a scrapbook with all your little cuttings in it—your football teams, your scholarships, your brilliance on every page. She told me you loved

toad-in-the-hole and roly-poly pudding, she told me
how wonderful you were, and she told me that I was
too young and unsuitable for her boy. She worshiped
you and now she is addicted to Ativan and sherry, she
can't sleep without barbiturates, because she gave her
entire life to two men who abandoned her and she is
nothing. "You wouldn't like me without my
tranquilizers," she shouted when I tried to confront
her about her drug addiction. She has nothing left Jack
and you know it.

But still you'd not admit it—you want a wife you
know is utterly devoted to you, whose life's work is
caring for her men as your mother did.

Admit it Jack. You get an erection when I take a
splinter out of your foot, when I squeeze your
blackheads or remove the wax from your ears.

Let's look at the last eight weeks. They build up to
your punishing decision. Examine it long and hard. I
realize you were drawing a map leading up to my
protesting release. Conscious or subconscious, the
scholarship boy was at the wheel.

Your company. Your company that I married into,
that I became first lady of. I always had a job in that
company and I did it well. Large as the firm was, I
maintained a family feeling. I kept my tentacles
reaching out to all the offices across the country. I
knew who was getting divorced, having an affair,
losing their grip. I knew whose children were off-the-
wall, who not to trust and who you should watch for.
I could see things that you couldn't, smell out trouble.
I gave dinners where I knew the businessmen's names

and their wives' professions, where the food and the flowers had style. I looked good and you were aware that I had given your firm a cachet it had lacked. When you finally decided to open an office in London, we started that office from scratch. You answering the phone and me decorating the hovel on a budget of a couple of hundred pounds. Cautious Jack, even though the firm was worth many millions— just in case it didn't work out.

And I went to secondhand office suppliers and watched their faces fall when they came to see the premises. I was embarrassed and used to make excuses, telling them how huge the firm really was, and how it would be so here.

Together we did it. We entertained and I introduced you to the right people in London and your first job, your first biggy, came through me. God, it was exciting, wasn't it Jack?

So what happened? What went wrong? As the offices grew, you opened ones in Paris, Hamburg, and Madrid. In London we moved from one building to another, each one slightly grander than the last. Until two months ago. The ultimate. What's more it was my old agent's office. I had gone there fearful ten years ago and now it was ours. So, so grand and affluent.

You said you wanted an office-opening party and at the same time you hired a new office manager. What happened Jack? Did you forget to tell her that I had a job? That I was active, very active in the company? When I asked her if she would like to come with me to choose the invitations for the office opening, she arrived one hour late, making me late for breast-feeding Sam. She used to get the receptionist to call me with "Just a moment, I have Patsy on the line" and I'd wait for five or seven minutes while she felt important. One day I came into the office and it was being redecorated. Top to bottom. Refurnished and refurbished.

She was standing in the hall.

"Yes, I'd like that color for the ceiling and the same for the woodwork."

I went to your office.

"Jack, that's my job—I didn't even know you were redecorating."

"Look Molly, we've been too busy to deal with this out of the office—she's on the spot."

Then she fired a lot of the office staff. My friends and allies. The receptionist, the secretaries, and she started to bring in her team.

I would telephone to speak to you and they'd say, "Who's calling?"

"Molly," I'd reply.

"Molly who?" they'd ask.

When I arranged to meet my florist and caterer a week or so before the party, I called to tell her.

"Why on earth tomorrow?" she asked.

"Because that's when we can do it," I replied.

"But won't everything have spoiled?"

She treated me like a fool. And when I did arrive with these people, she took over. Marched forward and said, "Now what I want is . . ." and once again I went to you Jack and I said, "Jack, that woman is

driving me crazy. Please would you tell her that she
should work *with* me."

And you sighed and stretched and lectured me
saying, "Now Molly, if you're not grown up enough to
handle a simple office manager, then I can't help you.
You know she's very good at her job and I'm not
going in there saying 'now you be nice to Molly.'"

"No Jack, I don't mean that. But she's getting away
with treating me like shit because no one has said to
her 'that's Molly's job' or 'listen, Molly's okay, she
knows what she's doing and she's an asset to this
company, let her help you.'"

But you wouldn't, would you Jack, so she took my
job.

The office was decorated by her. New paintings
chosen and hung by her. The party arrived and when
I came through the door she shook my hand and said,
"Welcome to MRL."

And all the while you mingled with your guests and
that bitch stood by the door in her strapless evening
dress, like the office wife, shaking people's hands and
saying, "Welcome to MRL."

I went to you and I said, "Surely Jack, we should be
standing by the door welcoming people?"

But you took no notice and when I told her there
was no paper in the lavatory, she looked at me and
said, "You know where it is."

I sought you out and told you I was leaving, and
amid three hundred people telling the office manager
how beautiful the flowers were, and how amazing the
food was, I left and you didn't even try to stop me.

WORKING FOR LOVE

You did ask me not to cry on the pavement in case your guests saw.

The next night I gave a dinner for ninety-four people. All your European professionals. I seated each person next to someone from a different office, I knew all their names. I was witty, and the evening was a raging success. I glowed because I knew how pleased you were and I knew that you would get up and make a speech. I knew you would thank me profusely and they would all clap.

I hope no one was looking at me when you stood up and spoke, as I realized that your speech was finished and you hadn't even mentioned my name.

You thanked your office manager for organizing such a good party the night before.

Later, as I showed the office manager our house, she stopped at a photograph of me taken when I was a model.

"You used to be quite glamorous, didn't you?" she said.

Much later, when they piled into the silly double-decker buses she had hired, that had broken off all the branches up my lane and driven over our neighbor's lawn, I started again, didn't I Jack? "Don't you realize she's taken my job, and none of you, not one of you, has supported me? No one stopped her, no one suggested she include me, no one told her of my role. You all let her do it. She is totally subservient to you men. You feel important every day. But I felt important in your company through my work and now I've been made redundant."

"Molly, I can't help the way you feel about yourself."

And on it went, didn't it? All night I tried to make you understand.

The next day I felt guilty. Guilty that I had kept you up so late when you had meetings.

I went out and bought you a beautiful cigar case. It cost £200. Then I bought champagne, caviar, and candles. I prepared a wonderful romantic dinner. When you came home I gave you the present.

"I'm sorry I complained so much," I said.

You loved the cigar case. You loved your dinner and you loved going upstairs and flopping out in front of the television and falling asleep. But I was good. I will not complain, I kept saying to myself. He is tired, he needs to unwind.

The following evening we had Babs, Meriel, and Carol to supper. Remember? It was all going so well.

Then you turned to me. In front of my girlfriends and you said, "Oh, by the way Molly, I'm taking that cigar case back."

"Why?" I was stunned.

"Because it's too extravagant, you can't go around spending money like that."

I took the plates into the kitchen and I heard you say to my friends, "She thinks she can just go and spend three thousand pounds without thinking."

chapter

8

I stood in my white an-
tique lace nightie as chaos billowed around me.
Chaos made of ice, chaos in black and white that
turns to fuzz, like the television after closedown. I
remember, I remember flattening myself against the
wall as the ambulance men came up the stairs with a
stretcher. Invisible, I stood and watched my beloved
elder sister carried down. Sheets, I remember white
sheets and white faces and the feeling, the same feeling I had two years before in the middle of the street
in New York. It was a whirling sensation: first your
emotions and instincts become acute—the adrenaline spurts through your body, whatever is happening you know is way past your control or anyone's but

here you stand watching; then suddenly it goes blank, you become limp—as if your body and mind went into overload, and rather than explode, the fuse cuts out.

Mary was placed in the ambulance. My father turned to the doctor.

"Can I follow with you in your car?"

"Actually, I'm going on to a dinner party, so you'll have to take your own," he said.

My mother went in the ambulance. My father followed.

In the morning Mathew and I went into our nanny Jenny's bed. Tumbling on the bed, playing hide-and-seek between the blankets. Being tickled and giggling until it ached.

"How's Mary?" I asked.

"You must ask your mother," said Jenny.

On we went, squealing with delight.

I can see her now, today, as if it happened hours ago. My mother walked in in her nightie. Her blue, voluminous negligee. Her hair was red in those days, her skin was very white.

"How's Mary Mummy?" I asked.

The words, the exact words I will hear forever.

"We must all be very brave. Mary died last night."

We didn't ask how or why or for any details you would expect.

Family lore says I responded thus: "Does that mean I can have her toys?"

I don't believe I said that, because I remember that whole day vividly, but it is what I was always told.

A death in the family to a young child is not an earth-shattering event. They cannot grasp it, take hold of it and understand it. It's more a now-you-see-it-now-you-don't situation. Life goes on; the devastation is beyond a small child's comprehension. What affects the child is the reaction of the parents. There is not one thing in the world that could be more horrible, more horrendous to both mother and father, than the death of one of their children.

There I was, watching these people I loved so dearly suffer. Their suffering was all-consuming.

My father was beyond help. He could not speak for grief. I remember vividly seeing his beautiful blue eyes fill with tears. I saw him weep in his bedroom, and then when he noticed me he asked me to leave. (I think it was around this time that I became a listener, or to put it more bluntly, an eavesdropper. I knew that there were things happening in this house that I didn't understand and perhaps if I listened, I could discover the secrets, see if I could do something, or if it was my fault.)

These people were inconsolable. They could not help each other, either. So my beautiful mother threw herself into her work, relentlessly, not stopping for a minute, not allowing herself four seconds to think her thoughts for fear that they would engulf her—and she would be drowned in her sorrow.

My father developed terrible pains in his chest and doctors from London came to see him.

"He has a broken heart," they told my aunt (my

mother was at work). "We now fully acknowledge this condition in the medical profession. Only time can cure it, if it cures at all."

So there we were. Our shining family reduced to my father with a broken heart, my mother, disappeared to work, my brain-injured brother, the guilty nanny, Jenny, and me.

Yes, me. I watched. I watched Mary's possessions being lovingly stored in a cedar chest. Her toys were given to her best friend. (I admit to being most put out about that.)

Somewhere in there I realized that the only way I could get my parents' attention was to plug into their grief. To become one of them. I don't think I actually rationalized it like that, but instinct told me.

I used to lie awake at night, waiting for Mummy to come in.

"I can't sleep Mummy, I keep thinking how sad I am about Mary."

She would hold me and tell me how sad she was, too, and then she would let me put on my dressing gown and take me outside where Daddy would be nurturing Mary's garden—a little patch six feet by six feet that he and she had been turning into a tiny paradise. Every night he would tend it, not allowing these little flowers she had planted to die too. I would sit and watch Daddy with his small trowel. Five acres we had, but only this little square was he interested in. He was consumed by it—frightened to let go of the last living part of her. His enormous hands holding a small fork, delicately weeding, forbidding the plants to die.

Instinct started to hint at lots of things. I had learned that our lives could no longer be the same. That just being the old Molly I was, didn't work. There wasn't time or energy for the normal. Our family had overtaken that and now, to be noticed, it had to be dramatic. To be cast in this tragedy you had to play the part. I couldn't sleep. That one worked. So they had to take me to a doctor. I was prescribed sleeping medicine.

"Poor Molly" (I would be sitting on the stairs listening), "I don't think we realized how deeply she was affected. We must give her more time."

And thus we spiraled into a drum, a deep hole, a crevasse of guilt, manipulation, and pain.

I craved attention, I craved approval, and I wanted to make them happy again. I started trying to do the things she did. But she did them so well.

We had to face the drive to school again. Term had started. There I was in the front, a poor substitute. I would search my mind for questions to ask my father, aching for him to respond.

"Now that's a very intelligent question, Molls."

I was listening, as usual, fighting off the sleeping medicine. Searching for clues.

They were fighting.

"Stop it, stop it Rachel, stop talking about it."

She was crying.

"But we did, we did, oh Christ we should never have spanked her as often as we did."

Small things, little incidents in a normal childhood became atrocities to haunt them.

I got some clues. I discovered that to get attention you need to die, or at least be gravely ill. I learned that to be noticed you had to have a problem, a serious problem. But most of all, I discovered that it was entirely my job to make them love me; I had to fill the void that she had left. I must live up to the heroine that she was in life and death.

My poor, sad parents. My wonderful parents who could not help their grief. Believe me, they were outstanding parents. I still think they were. They didn't know they had underestimated me. They tried their best. We were all trying our best.

And one day, on the way to school, finally, at last, it was said. What we all had really known, what we were all really thinking. I'm glad he said it. Even though I know it has pained him for the rest of his life. But it mustn't pain him because he had to say it, he had to release the monster that was slowly devouring him.

"Sing Molls sing. Sing like Mary did, sing about the trees and the fields and the woods."

And I tried. I desperately wanted to do it well. I spent nights afterward thinking of what I should have sung. But it was pathetic. I can see it now. I even know exactly where we were. Turning right by the Plough pub.

"Oh, the fields and the trees and the grass and the cows . . ."

"No, no, no," he shouted. Exhausted, at last he let go.

"Why can't you be more like her? Why can't you sing like her? The woods, the walks, the spark, you haven't got it, have you? Why can't you be her?"

chapter
9

You haven't telephoned me Jack. I'm leaving tomorrow and you haven't called. I've thought you had a number of times. But each time it was someone else.

I've had a wonderful holiday. On my own. You know, I think I've had a better time than any of the women here who are part of a couple.

God, there are some unhappy women existing in designer clothes. Each has told me her story. Each one is incredulous that there is life on your own—that a fellow member of the club could manage without her spouse, and dare to be alone.

We've forgotten, us mothers and wives, what it's

like to be by ourselves. For some reason, propaganda
has made us believe that it's a dark, empty crevasse.

Well, it is, if you feel like a dark, empty crevasse,
down deep in your soul.

Why were we all brought up to think that our
ultimate goal was to ensnare a partner and surround
ourselves with children? Then we would never be
lonely again. Bullshit, I've been loneliest since I've
been married.

What was happening when we grew up that made
us all think that a successful partner, a good strong
man, could make us happy? So I (and many millions
of others) looked long and hard for our salvation. This
demigod who would make us complete. I firmly
believed that total fulfillment would be achieved and it
would all be all right once I became a Mrs.

Why didn't anyone tell us that only one person can
make you happy and that's you? That only when you
feel total peace with yourself will you feel it with a
partner. That fulfillment and satisfaction are not things
your husband can dish out like merit points at school.
Why weren't we pushed toward careers and academic
achievements rather than husbands?

These husbands who find themselves strapped to a
woman, bending like a willow, waiting for this
promised bliss that isn't happening. And so the
woman thinks she's doing something wrong and he
feeds the fear. For years a wife tries to believe that
she has it all. A successful husband, a pretty house,
shiny children. But she feels empty. Why? Eventually
she has to face up to the fact that this union is not

41

what she was promised. Where is the warm glow of satisfaction? Oh, she has failed. Can she admit that she is unhappy?

Confused, filling with resentment and fear, she panics. Maybe has an affair, turning once again to someone else to make her happy. Money, ahh, what about the money? She has never earned a proper living.

Every woman at this hotel (six in all) has a variation of this story.

Four of the husbands are actively having affairs and their wives cling on.

And poor Phoebe. I watch her and know her husband is slipping away. She has a desperate quality; I can smell it, so can he. Phoebe, who puts on her makeup and walks on her toes, who looks at her husband at ten o'clock and says, "Shall we go to bed?" and he orders another drink.

I'm dancing to another tune and what a dance I'm doing. And guess what? I don't want a man within spitting distance. A long mirror would be more useful. To see for myself that I look pretty. For now, I stand precariously on a chair trying to see my whole self in the little wall mirror. I get a better picture and know it's true. At least if I topple, I topple alone. Don't get me wrong, I don't spend hours gazing at myself, only once a day after I've dressed for dinner. But Jack, I can't help wondering if I've lost my looks. The mirror says I haven't, but your behavior reflects a different picture.

Did my cunt get too loose after three babies? Was

that it? After all, the mirror couldn't verify that. I did
my exercises, I really did. But still it's not what it was,
is it? Breast-feeding those babies doesn't do a lot for
bosoms either. They've shrunk and when I cup my
hands around them they feel hollow. Lacking firmness,
no longer pert. My thighs wobble—no, worse, they
ripple.

I had a boyfriend I loved very much, the one I met
before you, and he once sent me a card: it said, "Arse
gone, tits gone, but there's still one hell of a lot left."
That was two babies ago. But there is *still* one hell of
a lot left and I shall dance my jig alone and love it. I
shall discover my talents. The time has come to
realize the hidden beauty.

The surface is not what it was and won't last
forever.

If I were ever in a car crash and had scars all over
my face, then my life would change. I am preparing
myself. It is time to learn to live without skin-deep
love. If you've been beautiful, as I once was, then it
comes as a great shock when as your looks dwindle,
so does the attention you've generated. The time has
come to find out what's inside. The outside is getting
worn—the inside will do the opposite; every day it
will shine more. But for me Jack, not for you.

chapter
10

There we were. Trying to cope with living. Desperate, each in our own way.

My mother was trying to get pregnant and had been since Mary's death. Grief blocked the way. My father was a frame, being eaten away slowly by sadness and guilt. Mathew was a little boy with brain damage and I was a little girl with brain damage. My father fought constantly with himself. Trying to come to terms with the fact that Mary was dead and I had lived.

It's a blur, that whole period. Children are very clever—they have a built-in protective device and when something begins to hurt too much they simply wipe it from memory. It doesn't mean that the mind hasn't absorbed it but that it has chosen to obliterate it from the archives.

My father built a rock garden on Mary's grave. The grave consisted of two plots instead of one and every day he was down there planting and tending. A gravestone arrived. No one could bear to even look at it, so they covered it and put it in the garage, where it has been ever since.

Mary's paintings were framed and hung in the house. Her poems were too. The local church was given two twelfth-century wood carvings in her memory.

My parents donated a silver cup to my school. It was called "The Mary Cup." It sat in a case and was to be awarded to the best high-jumper each year. Every day I would walk past it, gaze with fascination, and marvel at the glamor of having a trophy named after my sister.

My mother became the stronger member of the couple. My father could not function and my mother, realizing the need for solidarity, rallied herself. For about a year she held our family together with grim determination.

She became religious. I remember her confirmation.

A wonderful thing happened at the end of that year. My mother gave birth to a perfect baby girl. I stood with my father in the garden.

"What will you call the baby Daddy?"

"Meriel."

"Oh, that's lovely."

"Yes, I thought it was like Mary."

And he believed that the new Mary had been born and from that day he placed all his hopes in Meriel as he started to pull himself back together.

chapter
11

Suddenly, I have started to ache Jack. I have released
a part of me that has been sealed tight for a long time.
I have just allowed myself to feel. I am crying; the
tears flow from my eyes like a dam that has burst. A
crater has exploded in my gut and at last I feel the
truth. I am aching, I am yearning for love. To be
touched, to be held. I long for arms to embrace me.
For the closeness and care. Where has it gone? Oh,
hollow chest at last released, no longer tight but open
with honest emptiness. Today I discovered the truth. I
suppose my body and mind have decided I'm ready
for it. Why have I been deprived of the attention I
deserved for so long?

When Sam was born, that is when the ache really

started. I watch the video time after time. Six months ago, there we are in the hospital, you behind your camera. Safe, detached, protected by this machine, and I delivered you a son. Your first son. A perfect boy. And you remained behind your camera for forty minutes afterward. I kept looking at the lens to talk to you. It's there on film, I am talking to a camera.

"A boy Jack, a boy, a boy."

"Yes Molly, well done."

You did not put down your camera for one minute to embrace me, to hold me, or look at your son. You stayed in your corner, filming. I needed you. It was my finest moment.

"The foot is fine," said Dr. Roberts.

"The foot's okay Jack, it's really fine."

Take me back to my sixth month of pregnancy when we went to have a scan and the doctor took an overlong look at the baby's foot. My radar picked it up. I asked.

"Your baby's foot seems to be particularly turned in and I think it might be talipes."

Our baby had a clubfoot. Or so the ultrasound examination informed us.

We left, I was weeping. You turned to me and said, "Molly, you cannot expect to go for a scan to be reassured that everything is normal. You have to accept the consequences. You've asked to be told and now you know, so stop making a fuss."

On and on you went, lecturing me.

Yet we both went for the scan expecting to have fun seeing a lovely, healthy baby and you knew it. But

would you accept a minute amount of responsibility?
Could you, could you have held me tight and told me
not to worry or said that this was our problem and
together we would cope with it?

No, you went back to your office and left me on
the pavement, weeping. Later that day, they arranged
for me to have another scan to double-check. I asked
you to come but you said you were too busy. That
scan also said that the baby's foot was talipes and I
called you and I said, "I'm glad we know Jack,
because now we are prepared for it. Otherwise the
discovery would mar the entire wonder of the birth.
We can find out now the best way of treating it and
then when the baby arrives it can be helped
immediately."

"Okay Molly, yup, that's fine."

But it wasn't, was it? Because you were distressed
you chose to show no support. Occasionally you
would lecture me and so I did my usual playacting.
Pretending I wasn't worried at all, because you would
not allow me to be upset. What right had I to be
upset when I had elected to have a scan?

Do you remember two weeks before the birth you
said, "This is going to be an exciting couple of
weeks."

"Why, darling?" I asked—praying for the sign of
interest.

"Because Gibsons are trying to take over McGregor
Boyall," you replied.

Another day, responding to my question "You're not
really interested in this baby, are you?" you said,

"How can I be interested when we had one only sixteen months ago?"

And there, my darling husband, there I lay in my nakedness. With my legs apart after sixteen hours of labor and I gazed at you, I beseeched you with my eyes. The longed-for son. I had been so frightened it would be another girl and that you would be upset.

And I said, "It's a boy and the foot is fine. Two miracles, two miracles." And you stayed behind your camera. At last, six months later I have erupted with sorrow and now I carry an empty chasm. But Jack, I shall fill it. I shall, slowly, because I have decided that I deserve to be loved and this test, this test of unhappiness I am faced with at last is your loss, not mine.

chapter

12

I loved my father more and more each year. I loved him with a passion that I have never known since. It was the love of a person who could never satisfy her beloved. It was unquenchable. It was a striving emotion that was bottomless.

When I was nine our relationship changed forever and my childhood ended.

We were in California. Living in a rented house. My mother was suddenly a very big star and we were there because she was making a movie.

Our lives had changed. We had two nannies and a cook. For a while we were Hollywood children. Mixing with stars and swimming in the kidney-shaped pool. It was fun. Everyone was happy. My father was becoming very famous too. Mathew was miraculously recovering and our new baby was perfect.

One evening Mummy came home. She had a headache.

"Please Mummy, will you bathe me?" I begged.

She came upstairs and started to talk to me while I washed. She started to sway.

"Molly, I've got a terrible pain, I'll have to go and lie down."

I knew, I knew as I sat in the water, my tummy in little rolls and my white thighs covered in bubbles, that a massive and horrific thing was going on. I could feel it, sense it. I had grown a strong sense of impending disaster, my instincts had become finely tuned to pick up a whiff of the dramatic. I began to feel the adrenaline surge through me. I ran to the stairs and called to Daddy, who sauntered up, martini in hand.

"What is it Molls?" he asked.

"Look." I led him by the hand to the bedroom door and there on the bed lay my mother. Covered in vomit and unconscious.

"Go back to the bath," he ordered.

I plonked myself in the tepid water and listened to the commotion in the room next door. Listen—oh, how I listened. An event I wanted to be a part of was taking place. My beautiful mother, what was happening to her?

My father was on the telephone.

"She's unconscious now, but she's been asking the names of the people in the house."

My nanny came in and wrapped me in a towel and hustled me through the bedroom while I strained to see my mother again. She put on my nightie and left me in my room. I sneaked back and listened at my parents' bedroom door. All was silent. I crept back to my room. Mathew was being brought to bed and was about to be read a story. The wail of an ambulance siren came toward us through the night.

"What's that?" asked Mathew.

"It's a cat," said the nanny.

"No, it's not," I said. "It's an ambulance coming for Mummy." They came again. There I was, pressed against another wall, in another country, watching, invisible. They ran up the stairs this time. Noise, oh, so much noise. Machines, they had machines that hissed, breathed, lights flashed, their teeth flashed. American ambulance men with glinting stretchers— no wooden poles like our little English ones. I watched, once again in my nightie, as this cyclone of machinery and men maneuvered my beautiful, glamorous mother, covered in sick and mumbling, down our pink marble Hollywood staircase. For the third time in my life I watched a beloved member of my family being loaded into the greedy, open mouth of an ambulance. The siren started to wail, the doors closed, and the performance was over. My mother, my father, and the gleaming men disappeared and I stood at the window, watching the neighbors go back into their houses, shutting their doors, and I gazed at the mysterious glinting lights of what Mummy called "downtown Hollywood."

chapter
13

Okay Jack, I'm home. I had a wonderful holiday and I'm home. Your body is imprinted on my bed, your dirty mugs sit in my car, and your shirts are lying on the floor in the bathroom. Yet you, you left this morning because you knew I was coming home.

Well shit on you, as my mother would say.

Daisy said, "Shall I call Daddy and ask him where the doll Eileen bought for me is?"

"Yes darling, why don't you?"

So she called you at our house in London and there was no answer. So she called your office and there was no answer.

I felt like I had ants running through my veins.

"Try the house again." I went on reminding her to

keep trying all day and there was never any answer.
Where were you? It occurred to me that you might be
doing it on purpose. Knowing that I was home and
using your silence as a lever to undermine me.

Because you can be that cruel can't you Jack?
When I'm at my peak, my strongest peak, you can
destroy me with expertise. You *could* destroy me with
expertise. Not today, you won't. The glory of my
holiday is not yours to mangle.

Miscarriage had followed miscarriage. I had learned
to expect the joy to be obliterated within six weeks. I
grew to fear the sudden flow to red blood, heralding
another dying embryo. And you would not let me cry.

"Don't feel sorry for yourself Molly. You've got to
be brave."

Four years it took me, four years to conceive
Gwennie. As I lay in bed in hospital, five weeks
pregnant and bleeding, you came to my bedside.
There I was, glowing with joy. Filled at last with a
chance of motherhood, of having your baby, at last I
was getting medical help.

And you would be so thrilled and proud of me. Dr.
Roberts had told us that I should remain as calm as I
could. "No upsets, no moving."

You pulled your chair right up beside me and
looked into my eyes. "I've been thinking Molly."

"Yes Jack, what?"

"I've been thinking that this can't be my baby."

Total panic filled me. You turned to fuzz in front of
me. My eyes went warm and floaty. My entire glory,
the acute happiness, the overwhelming excitement,

was exploding inside me, being shattered into thousands of pieces that were tearing my insides. Making me feel sick.

"How can you say that?"

"Well, I've worked out the dates; there is no way you could have conceived this baby when we made love—you conceived this baby when you were in New York and I wasn't there."

"I didn't Jack, I've never slept with anyone but you since I met you. I promise you, you know that."

"But you had dinner in New York with Max, you went to see him in his play on your own."

"But I had dinner with him before the show, I didn't even see him after it."

"All right, tell me exactly what happened." And I told you. Exactly what happened. I had supper with him, my old friend, an actor whose wife is an even better friend, and then I saw his play and then I went home, alone. But you didn't believe me. I begged you to. I sobbed. I became hysterical, while you sat there calmly. Watching me. Newly pregnant with a baby we had been trying to have for four years. Blood dripping from my vagina, warning us that I could lose my precious fetus.

Every day you would come to my bed and say, "Tell me exactly what happened again."

I would tell you. Then you would say, "Your story has changed."

And you would pull out some minute detail. As the days wore me down, my euphoria lost forever, bleeding becoming heavier, I forbade you to visit me.

"You are destroying me and my baby. I have let you destroy me but you are not going to get my baby. You have no right to doubt me, no right to treat us like this. Please do not, do not, come and see me again until you can forget this whole fucking stupid business."

You said you were sorry and that you believed me. But it was too late. We didn't share the passions of parents expecting their first child, the excitement of the anticipation. It had been shot, very accurately, by you.

The seven months following were sad. I feared that our baby would not look like you. That our baby might look like Max and we would be back in the murky pond of doubt, questions, and denials.

Oh, we should have been so happy. Gwennie was born on June twenty-second. The total image of you. "Jack in a dress" we call her now. She bore no resemblance to me at all. In fact I questioned who her mother was.

chapter
14

W_e didn't see Daddy for three or four days after the ambulance had whisked him away. We didn't see Mummy for three or four weeks. Millie, a friend of my parents', had come to me the next morning and told me that Mummy was "not very well."

As if I didn't know. No one else said anything. I was taken out of school because the gates were lined with reporters asking questions and wanting to take photographs of me. I thought it was rather exciting. We mooched around our house for two or three days, the cook, the nanny, and the three children, a protective barrier surrounding us. No one going out and the occasional friend coming in to "visit the children."

My father returned exhausted. I can hold the moment now. I can relive him opening the door and standing in the marble hall. His face was gaunt and he needed to shave. His shoulders had given up and his eyes were disappearing. His body hollow, his long cardigan open, and I ran to him—at least the ambulance hadn't stolen him from me. But he was tired, oh, so tired. He went upstairs, bathed, changed, and slept.

Later, when he came downstairs, there was no time for stories. He simply explained that Mummy was very, very ill and he had to spend most of his time with her. Our cook and nanny would look after us. He was overwhelmed and his air of deep unhappiness was as vivid as his red cardigan.

And I, aged nine, would wander around the dark, thick-carpeted house. I couldn't quite work it out. Mummy was clearly not well, but what was "not well"? Was it tummy or head or broken bones? Mathew was apparently not well, but he could walk and talk and even though he occasionally had to be rushed to the hospital and everyone worried about him, he seemed all right to me.

Mary hadn't been well, I could see that, but then she died and never came home. But all these people consumed my father's every moment. Every time we were nearly a normal family, something else happened that took him away from me. Every time I thought he was about to have time for me, he was grabbed from my grasp. But why? What was going on that I could not be a part of? This glorious man, my life and love who was never quite within my reach. Who I could never quite fascinate or please, and whenever we were about to get a chance to know each other he was called away to another tragic member of the family.

"Your mother is off the critical list," the cook said one morning. I had a vision of the critical list being something published in papers like Births, Deaths, and Criticals. "Off the critical list"—and what did that mean?

"It means she is not going to die," said the cook.

My father was coming home more. He started to talk to me as if I were a grown-up. I didn't realize that I had become the second most grown up in the family.

"Mummy is getting better and guess what, she's expecting a baby."

This was news indeed. Perhaps all this illness was to do with that. No one told me that my mother had massive brain damage. My mother had had three strokes, they told me.

I had looked knowledgeable and nodded. Being treated like a grown-up was fun and as long as I acted like one, Daddy would continue this new intimacy I was enjoying.

No one told me that my mother could not talk, could not move her right side, had no hair, had a crooked mouth. Someone could have stopped to explain to me that she wore an eye patch and didn't even know how to say my name. But no one thought of it.

The enormous excitement I felt when Daddy told me that Mummy was well enough for a visit surged through me. I counted the days. I sat in the front seat beside him. Feeling proud. It was the first time we'd driven together since Mummy went.

"Should I mention the baby?" I asked.

"I don't think so," he replied.

My beautiful mother. Soon, soon I would be beside her and she would be laughing and cuddling me like she used to. I could tell her all about the beastly nanny and missing school and the reporters.

We walked together along the hospital corridors. Here I was, alone with Daddy, I, the grown-up, no one else had been allowed to come. A skip every few steps was the only thing that revealed my age. There we were outside her door.

"You go in alone Molly, give her a surprise," he said.

So I turned the handle and opened the door. I put my head around first, with a huge grin, and said, "Surprise!"

Surprise is not exactly the emotion that comes to me as I remember those seconds. Horror, fear, nausea, yes, all those. Nothing and no one had remotely prepared me for what I saw. This thing that was meant to be my mother. This woman propped up in bed with tubes coming out of every hole. But that was the best part. She had no hair, she had a black eye patch, she had lipstick smeared over a lopsided mouth.

I stood there paralyzed with fear. She lay there paralyzed. One side of her limp. Then she lifted one hand and held it up, and out of her crooked mouth came extraordinary childlike moans. Clearly she wanted me to come to her. Still I was outside the door with just my head sticking into her room.

She moaned again.

"Go on, go in." My father shoved me and pulled the door shut. I was alone, I thought, with this terrifying woman. Then I heard a voice.

"Look Rachel, here's Molly."

There was a nurse sitting at the side of the room with knitting on her lap. My relief when I saw her was indescribable.

Once more my mother put her hand up and moaned at me.

"Go and sit beside your mother Molly, she wants you to go to her."

There was nothing in the world I wanted to do less. All I wanted was to escape from this harpy.

But Daddy was clearly barring the door on the other side and anyway, wasn't I a grown-up?

I smiled.

"Hello Mummy," I whispered.

"Love, love, love." She strained the word from her throat and sounded like a deaf-and-dumb person trying to speak.

I went and sat beside her.

"Your mother's lunch will be coming soon, perhaps you'd like to feed her?" asked the nurse.

"Yes, that would be nice," I lied.

Nice? Nice? That would be a nightmare. That would be the most horrible, terrifying thing I could imagine, just as this entire experience is like a terrible joke. How could I have looked forward to something that has become the most devastating moment I can remember? But I am a grown-up, I thought. I must not show my horror, my fear, my disgust. I must help these people, my parents. My mother looked at me, then from deep down inside her belly came a raw cackle. She laughed and laughed—she clearly realized how revolted I was and this was her only way of expressing it. The door opened and in came a woman with her food.

"Ah, here we are Rachel, here's lunch. Now Molly, can you help me pull your mother up—that's right. No, now be careful of those tubes. One, two, three, pull, up we go. Let's put on Rachel's bib, so she doesn't dribble on her nightie. All right Molly, you put little mouthfuls on the spoon and feed Mummy."

"Right." I stood up and could hardly reach the bed table. So I stood on tiptoe, terrified I would topple over and knock one of the tubes out or, worse still, land on her.

Each mouthful was a year of our lives. I can see in retrospect that she was as humiliated as I was horrified. Chasing the peas around the plate, both of us giggling nervously. Oh God, oh God, it makes me go red and sweat and the tears still pour down my cheeks when I relive it.

But I did not cry then. Watching the jelly drip

down the limp side of her mouth onto her bib, I felt utterly miserable and alone, but I did not cry, not in front of her or Daddy. After all, they needed my support.

chapter

15

So it's not going as planned, is it Jack? I'm not lying on the floor hyperventilating and begging you to come back.

I'm doing rather well, thank you.

And you, now you've seen how I can manage without you,. you think that you can skip back into my life just as nimbly as you skipped out five weeks ago. Well think again, sunshine.

Oh how I laughed when you telephoned me and I laughed even more (never in front of you) when you came to "see the children," and I was getting ready to go out to dinner. Of course, I had nowhere to go, but the sheer irritation on your face as you saw me appear in contact lenses and makeup (and you know I don't put on either for just anyone) was worth at least a month of misery.

But you collected yourself pretty quickly and the only visible sign of displeasure was your jaw muscle in spasm as you stood looking at me. You noticed, I noted, that I was no longer wearing my wedding ring.

Then I said, "Good-bye darling, I have to rush, I'm late for dinner," as sweetly as ever I could, hopped in the car, and drove around the leafy lanes of Bucks for an hour. But it was worth it. You see my darling, funny, wonderful things are happening to me. Extraordinary changes are sprouting inside myself. You said when you left that I had to realize that I was responsible for my own unhappiness and that if you left, then I would realize that I was just as miserable alone and so I'd stop blaming you for what I am, because I'm like that anyway.

Oh sweet realization—you are wrong. I am becoming something I like. I am developing a confidence I never had before. For the first time in my life I have total control and no one around my neck to tell me what I'm doing wrong, I don't have to prove myself to anyone but me. I admit that I am motivated somewhat by a terrific anger that is stoking me up and pushing me.

But my need to achieve is a very exciting experience. To discover that perhaps being alone isn't so bad and even I can earn money. I wake at five-thirty nowadays. I write for an hour before I get dressed and then get the children up, breakfasted, and in their correct directions. What a mass of never-ending occupations takes up the next sixteen hours, and then I roll into bed and set the alarm for five-thirty again.

Meanwhile, you are smarting. You, who set your jaw and walked out five weeks ago with a look of total control on your face. You, who ate your three-course meal as you told me of our separation. You, who thought you had lifted me out of the gutter and given me financial standing.

I don't know why I think I should stick around. I just live in this eternal hope that one day you'll become that person you pretend to be. But it couldn't last, could it?

A day, a week, a month. You are a con artist. An actor. We all know what a penchant I have for actors.

You are a liar. A man of many guises. To onlookers the very essence of honesty. This open-faced northerner, tall and kind. So sensible, so rational: his wife, however, explosive, oversensitive. Oh no Jack. Underneath that surface calm, that understanding, understated chap is another person altogether. A tough, selfish manipulator.

No one makes the millions you've made, no one runs the business you run by being a splendid chap.

You hire, you fire. You ruin people and then sleep soundly. You can pass men with white sticks selling matches, viewing them cynically with your 20/20 vision.

You, who can pass dogs running in terror on the motorway. You, who can turn away black men at the door selling paintings, hardly giving them a second of

67

your precious time before you brush them off. You, who never drop a penny in a tin. Who never shudders at a child screaming with misery as its mother slaps it in the supermarket. You, who can read stories in tabloids of child abuse and then eat a hearty breakfast.

Oh, you laugh at me.

"You cannot suffer for the world Molly."

Oh no, but I can care.

I said that you were a con man. I was correct.

We moved to London five years ago. Our friends gasped. "What a wonderful man. How lucky you are to have a husband who will give up everything for his wife."

I thought you'd changed, that you'd decided to move to London because I was so unhappy in Manchester.

You moved to London to expand your business. You moved to London to make more money. You moved to London for a challenge. You moved to London to prove how brilliant you were. It was safe. You owned an enormous firm and you were simply expanding. But oh, how they applauded and gazed. This super chap, this excellent fellow, doing it all for Molls.

Just where did that leave Molls?

Under a heap of pressure, that's where. Grateful, oh, how grateful I was meant to be. Attentive, for I was nervous that you would feel emasculated. You had ventured onto my territory and I had to be careful not to make you feel insecure. Every party we went to was horrific. Every man I spoke to, you were suspicious of. Was he an old lover? Who were these people? How did you drive from one side of London to the other? You didn't. You would get lost time after time and I would say "sorry." A man who has to have total control, in unknown surroundings with unknown people.

Hell.

Once again you would come home with an air of displeasure. If I had a friend there, you would be furious. If I was on the telephone, it was a crime. Here you were, moved south to make your wife happy and it was all her fault. You worked from five A.M. to nine P.M. I could not complain about it. You would come home and collapse.

"For Christ's sake Molly, I'm doing this for you. Not me. Oh no, I don't want to live in your crummy city with all your pseudosophisticated ex-lovers. I'm doing it to make you happy."

I hated you. I used to fantasize about you dying. Then I would be free. Without the stigma of divorce. Widows are pitied. Widows are respectable, and widows inherit a lot of money.

I started to become frightened. Not of anything in particular. I started to be nervous. I became terrified of flying. I became scared of people. Business dinners became a nightmare. Soup was my dread. I would shake so much that the liquid slopped over the edge of the spoon—never reaching my mouth.

My already fragile sense of self-worth was drying out fast.

"Will nothing make you happy? Here I am in London," and on, and on. Wasn't I a wretch, wasn't I a leech? A spending machine. I had a nanny, I had a cleaning woman, I had you to dole out money when I asked nicely for it. What was I complaining about?

Drip, drip, drip. How to own your wife. Ignore, lecture, order, control, demand obedience, reject, put down, withdraw, dominate.

Drip, drip, drip.

"Oh your life's so tough isn't it?"

Very clever.

"Poor Molly, there's so much to complain about."

Drip, drip, drip.

Anger, frustration, anxiety, withdrawal, self-doubt, fear, insecurity, defiance, rebellion, self-hate, alienation, resentment, dependency, hostility, submission, compliance, and failure.

Psychiatric hospital.

"Poor old Jack."

"What he has to put up with."

"A failure as a wife. I have everything, everything a wife could ask for. A handsome, successful husband who loves me. A pretty house. A car to drive. A kind man who took both me and my daughter in. Who looks after us. Who puts up with me. Oh woe, what a failure am I."

The psychiatrists and counselors would look and nod as I told them what a disaster I was. We had group therapy every day. All women. All women of fifty and sixty. All women from Kent and Surrey and London. I looked at them with contempt. What have I got in common with these middle-class, menopausal victims? thought I. But I listened, I listened to their stories as they opened old scars. As their stitches were removed and the bile of their marriages emerged. A thread, I began to pick up a thread running through them all. Like the key game where you thread the string up skirts and down trousers as the party guests sit in a circle. We sat in our circle and one day I realized. No slow dawning. Not a gradual awareness. Yank, I pulled the string and joined them.

"I'm not very happily married," I said.

You see, I listened to these ladies. They were all very bright and yet they had all allowed themselves to be dominated by men who were really weaker than they were. They none of them had careers but had spent their lifetimes listening to men and children. A lot of them were expatriates, whose husbands had relocated time after time, and these women had found new homes and new friends every few years, while their husbands slipped comfortably behind new desks cushioned by secretaries. They had each and every one devoted themselves and now felt empty, angry failures.

This is me in thirty years, I said to myself. While Joyce told of her husband who lectured and patronized her for twenty years, all the while wondering why she was such a neurotic. Eventually, he persuaded her to have electric shock treatment for her depression. "Depression is anger turned inward," our counselor would tell us.

"You know, I've just realized that we don't have fun, Jack and I. We honestly don't ever go out and have fun. If Jack wants to have fun then he buys me

71

something lavish and then I'm meant to be
happy. . . ."

"You know, I've just realized that I'm frightened of
Jack. He intimidates me. . . ."

"You know, I've just realized that I've been
accepting the blame for everything. . . ."

"You know, I've just realized that I've allowed Jack
to dominate me for our every waking moment. . . ."

"You know, I've just realized that we have the
classic parent-child relationship. . . ." It's the I'm-
okay-you're-not-okay syndrome.

"But I am okay," I announced after two months
inside.

Slowly, slowly, I began to understand. I began to
realize that I couldn't go on allowing you to control
me, through your manipulation and constant put-
downs. But I also realized that I had to stop allowing
you to do it. Stop accepting the blame. A little seed
was starting to stir. A germ of realization. We had a
meeting. I said it straight. You said you understood.
We would work on our problems together.

Four days later we toppled. You accused me of a
crime so unjustified and untrue. You looked at me
with disdain, turning away as I broke into sobs,
begging you to believe my innocence. You, sighing,
turned on the television.

Snap.

"I don't need you. I don't need your constant
tyranny. All we have is money, nothing else. No
partnership, no caring, no sharing. I've done
everything to be what you want me to be. I've been

to shrinks, to counselors, to psychiatric hospitals. I've groveled, I've begged, I've been reduced to a pulp. For what? To make you feel important.

"I'm twenty-five and I'm miserable. We have no fun, we never giggle, we never just enjoy. Well, listen, I've had it. I've had enough. I was happier living in my little house with Daisy. I don't want to be married to you anymore. I've had enough of justifying my existence. I'm not doing it anymore. I'm leaving you."

You were a little amazed.

"Please don't go Molly."

"I've got to. For my own sanity. To preserve what sense of self I've got left."

"I'm sorry, I'll change."

"No you won't."

"I will, I really will. I love you Molly."

All night, all night the storm raged. Eventually I agreed to stay. And you said you would change. You would go and see a therapist, you promised.

Promises, promises.

I got pregnant after four years of trying. The doctors said, "It was your emotional lives preventing you from pregnancy. Now you are so much happier it will all be fine."

But pregnant women are vulnerable women and we all know you'd never miss a chance, would you?

So why did I stay? It was a bit like giving up smoking. As desperately as I wanted a cigarette, I wouldn't have one because I knew the agony I went through giving up was so enormous, I couldn't imagine ever going through it again.

Each time we had a rebirth of our relationship and you promised never to treat me badly, I knew that we had been through so much that it couldn't repeat itself and as desperately as I wanted to leave you, I couldn't because of the years of pain.

It has to get better. He has to mean it this time. No one, no one who can be so wonderful, so loving, and so kind can go rotten again. Surely he's learned this time. And you would wind me up. Give me a good shot of loving, caring, and joy and just as I was hooked, just as I was at the peak of happiness and had started to relax, you'd take me to the edge and watch me fall.

chapter
16

I did not visit Mummy in hospital again, it was not suggested and I was not about to bring it up.

I became incredibly spoiled. As my mother started to recover, friends began to dare to visit the children, and always with a present.

I was developing into a strange crossbreed of supportive adult and spoiled child. I did not go to school. People felt they had to be nice to me at all times.

My maternal grandmother visited and in between the trauma of meeting her daughter in a catastrophic state, she fawned over her grandchildren. Treats—it was treats for Molly. But always at the back of my mind I had a terrible fear. The fear of my mother coming home.

This hideous creature who cackled and moaned was one day coming back to live with us. I was terrified.

Days came and went. Movie stars came and went. They would drop by and have a drink and make a bit of a fuss of me. Mathew and the baby were nursery material. I was the lady of the house. I'd offer them a Scotch or gin, pour it for them, and make conversation that could fool any adult. Daddy liked it. He was pleased to see that I was surviving so well. He was relieved that I had become so mature. I became his woman. I would wait up at night for him and then listen to his day. I would fix little snacks and tell him what had happened at home.

We all waited. We all waited for Mummy to become well enough to travel back to England. The house that had once been so chic—so glamorous, with its marble staircase and thick carpets—was oppressive. Frank Sinatra had sent over his entire record collection with a very grand gramophone and it seemed that our every waking moment was accompanied by his voice.

" 'Trailer for sale or rent, room to let for fifty cents. . . .' " The nanny adored that one—over and over again it was played. The nanny, the cook, Mathew, Meriel, and me, and Frank Sinatra.

We lived our lives for four months, long enough for me, with help, to completely betray childhood.

I can remember the night she came home. The

first time ever I voluntarily went to bed early, before the ambulance had arrived. I heard it all. I heard them lifting her up the stairs. I cried, oh God, how I cried. While they laughed, there was so much bloody laughter.

In the morning I stood, paralyzed, filled with dread, not daring to open my bedroom door. Eventually I nudged it open, just a couple of inches. I saw a woman's head. Short hair, her back to me. Oh my God, how could I get downstairs without being seen by this terrifying woman, my mother?

There was a walk-in cupboard that went across the back of the landing. I hated it, but not as much as the idea of Mummy. I went through the bathroom and boldly into the dark. I worked my way past fur coats and net petticoats, mothballs and wool. It went on and on. I could feel the ripples of hanging clothes, the stumbling over shoes. And then the door handle and what if it was locked? I turned it and emerged into the chocolate-colored study at the other side of the house. My tunnel to freedom. The sunlit room. In my euphoria I hadn't noticed a thin curl of smoke coming from behind the large, high-backed leather chair.

"Who's that?"

He swiveled the chair around and looked amazed. There I stood, red-faced, having battled in the dark with hanging, empty clothes, suddenly thrust into light. Disheveled in my dressing gown.

"Molls, what are you doing here?"

"I didn't want to disturb Mummy on the landing."

"But Mummy's still asleep."

Tessa Dahl

"No, she's on the landing."

He stood up and walked toward me.

"That's her nurse, now let's go down and get you some breakfast." Daddy protected me all the way to the kitchen.

chapter
17

And so here we are my dear Jack, you have managed to squeeze your way back into my arms. How do I feel about it? I don't think I like you very much—I also think that I love you—I also know that I will never ever again allow myself to be treated as you have treated me in the past. But it is so exhausting, being a sentry officer guarding my self-esteem. Watching you, listening, and then catching you when you start an old game. This is hard work and yet I know that if we slide back into our old relationship, within three weeks we will have reverted to our old patterns.

But it worked, didn't it? You are panting at the back door. You are behaving as a suitor would. Why are you now treating me as I have longed to be? Does my independence turn you on?

Six weeks after you left me you made a date.

"Please could we have lunch?" you asked.

"Certainly, if you come here." I ordered and you came, in your suit, and I watched your every gesture, realizing that for the first time I had control.

You took me out to lunch, but the table the maître d' gave us was in the middle of the room—by the door—and unacceptable. So we got back into the car and drove.

"Well, it doesn't matter, we can drive around looking for somewhere and discuss what's happening," you said.

"I don't want to talk about the relationship."

"Why not?"

"Because I'm not ready to."

"What do you mean?"

"I mean that I am not going to discuss this relationship with you Jack, it's too soon."

"Don't be silly, we have to start sometime."

"*I* don't."

"Now Molly, don't be silly, surely the whole point of us meeting is to discuss our thoughts and plans?"

"Look Jack, you left me six weeks ago, you didn't call me for five weeks, now you think you can snap your fingers and I'll be there, waiting to chew over the subject of your choice. Well, I'm not. I'm not remotely ready. I don't know how I feel about this relationship yet and I will not discuss it."

WORKING FOR LOVE

Oh ho-ho Jack. That flummoxed you, didn't it? You took a long, deep, patient breath.

"All right, if you don't want to discuss it then I will."

"Fine."

So you started.

"I've been thinking about what I want from this marriage and I want to tell you, then you can tell me what you want. Okay?"

Silence. I was as tightly huddled as any person could be in the front seat of a BMW. My legs drawn in, my arms wrapped around them, examining my fingernails, pushing down the cuticles.

"I want someone who will care for me. I want someone who will love me. I want someone who can share my business life with me and be a support to my work and, most of all, I want a wife who is strong, who can manage on her own and who needs me for loving and caring and not to carry her through life. Now, what do you want Molly?"

"I don't want to talk about this relationship."

"Come on Molly, what was the point of us getting together if we weren't going to discuss our hopes and aims?"

"Jack, this is not a strategic-planning meeting."

"Okay, then I'll tell you something else."

"All right."

"I'll tell you that I miss you and that I love you."

No reaction.

"I'll tell you I'm very sad that you don't wear your

wedding ring anymore. Obviously you don't consider yourself married to me."

Silence.

"Now, what are you going to say?"

"I'm not going to say anything."

Then you got nasty. It was so predictable. You had to come through with the power—the wand—didn't you?

"Look, if you are not going to cooperate I'll have to tell you a few more things. It's all very well for you to think that I'm going to support you as normal. You can tell me that you stick to your budget and that I can trust you, but I've decided that is not acceptable. If you no longer consider yourself married to me, then we will have to work out some sort of financial arrangement because I can't just sit back and not know what's going on."

"You need to control it," I suggested.

"You're damn right I do."

The ice maiden, I still remained calm. A smirk crossed my face.

"Look Jack, you left me six weeks ago. You told me to try to manage on my own. Well, I'm doing just that —I'm only just starting to learn new things about myself and now you want to change the rules again. I can't talk about us, I'm only just starting on me. But if you feel that this is not acceptable to you, then contact my lawyer. Work out a financial plan."

That shocked you. You stopped that car and ripped off your wedding ring.

"Fine," you shouted, "I won't be married to you either."

And then you threw it down. Not a very effective gesture in a car.

I picked it up and sighed.

"Now come on Jack, calm down."

Then I reached over and touched your hand.

Oh Christ, oh my God. It happened, didn't it? One touch and the addiction came back to life. All the need and the wanting, all the love, the deep love, the caring.

But we didn't say anything—oh no, this was game time.

So we drove around aimlessly, a bit breathy, talking rubbish. Not wanting to go home and for it to end. We drove around and around. Eventually I said, "Let's find somewhere to park and I'll show you my holiday photos."

So we drove into the woods. You looked at my pictures.

There I was, having a good time, pretty, laughing, and you said, "Oh Christ, I'd forgotton how lovely it was there."

Me or Nevis?

Then you reached forward and cupped my face in your hands. You kissed me as I have never been kissed before. My entire soul started to waft and then drown in emotion. I was filled with a rawness, so needy and so longing. Days, weeks, months, and years of craving. All the emptiness begging for help

83

started to subside with that one kiss. Then, in silence, total silence, we drove home.

The children, our children, came running out to the car. We went into the house and all I could think of was my need to kiss again.

"Come and see Gwennie's new swimsuit," I said. You followed me upstairs and there we fell on each other again. As if it were the first time ever that we had touched.

"Will you have dinner with me tonight?" you asked.

Lunch, we never had lunch. We never had anything this wonderful ever.

I staggered through the rest of the day in a trance. We took the children riding and you kept looking at me.

"Are you okay Molly?" you'd ask.

Oh my God, the attention, the care, I was drowning in it. Lapping up every second of tenderness.

As suppertime approached a fear started to envelop me. Years of bad habits and neglect do not disappear with a kiss. However remarkable. I decided to get tough.

"I don't think we should have dinner Jack. I think we should call it a day while it's still good."

"Don't be silly Molly—we're both hungry—let's just go and eat. We don't need to talk."

So we did. Wary though—the drug was easing off and I was becoming realistic. We got back to the house and I looked at you and said, "I don't want you to think that today has changed anything."

And you replied, "Of course not, it's hardly going to alter the world."

Then a voice from some little corner of my body, some instinctive part of my being way beyond my control, said, "Well, it's changed my world."

I must have entwined myself around you, aching for love as no one had ever done before. That kiss was even more remarkable, the world was bursting with years of unsung care. We went into the house and I said, "Jack, I'm not going to sit for days telling you what a shit you've been, but I do have to exorcise my immense anger. You have to hear my feelings, you have to realize what has happened. While you've been away I've started writing a story, and now I'd like you to come and listen."

So we went upstairs and I blushed for an hour while I read it to you. You sat in total silence.

At the end you looked at me and said, "I'm sorry."

chapter
18

With an enormous send-off and fanfare we left America and returned to England.

I felt suffocated by babies. Mathew was still treated like one, Meriel was one, Mummy couldn't talk or walk or read or write or do anything, and to make matters worse, not only was she a baby but she was about to have one.

Once again everyone but me needed attention. I couldn't even be the sophisticated lady anymore. This was England. Our old rambling farmhouse. My friends and cousins and aunts, no one would let me get away with pouring gins for visitors and dining alone with Daddy. What was I? A misplaced little fat thing. A spoiled girl, who had been showered with attention, but now usurped. Daddy, my Daddy who I helped through this hideous crisis, had forgotten me, so many worries had he. Would the baby, expected imminently, be all right? Could Daddy pay the massive hospital bills that poured in from America? Now he had to support the family.

Mummy was everyone's focal point. This woman, who would drag her leg around and wear an eye patch. This mother of mine, carrying a vast swollen belly that made her topple over like a Kelly doll. She would shout and scream. Make up words that we didn't understand and then laugh hysterically. Every day swarms of visitors would come and sit with her. On my father's instructions they would make her study, like a kindergarten child, reading, writing, and arithmetic. Mathew was more advanced at school than she was.

We were like an orchestra, a very battered orchestra with an enormous, powerful, and determined conductor struggling to make us survive. This extraordinary household filled with people, needing. All crying, all babies, and some needing far more help than others. Of course, there was only one answer for me. I chose a role that made me needed too. I became a mother.

I tended and cared and bathed and fed. I washed and dried each one in turn, including my mother. I dressed and undressed each one in turn, including my mother. And when my mother went away to have her baby, I prepared the baby's room with all the love and attention of a parent.

I knew her baby would be normal. I visited them every day and always sat possessively holding my new sister.

If I had had a breast, I would have placed the nipple between her lips and let her suck.

She was mine. I went to the village bookshop and bought a baby book and filled it in. This baby was going to have a proper mother who could do it like normal mothers did.

When I came home from school I would read to all my babies. I would read to my mother and then to Mathew and then to Meriel and play with baby Fanny. Oh, the responsibilities of motherhood. So much to do, so many tasks—a woman's work. And where was Daddy? No longer driving me to school, no longer collecting me. Those precious times were past. Other parents—a school run. Where was the other grown-up in the family? Look at me Daddy, shall I make this home a normal one? Yes, I shall help you.

All this crying will stop, for I can care for these babies. These four bodies in our way, who make you look so tired and worried, who demand your every waking moment, together we will nurse them and make it all right.

We are a pair, and you need me. I will be a good replacement, Daddy.

But then the grown-ups interfered. They poked their long noses in and said, "This is not right."

"This is not a childhood."

"This is unnatural."

"She needs to be with other children."

Within a week the divorce took place and you got custody, care, and control of my children. I was sent to boarding school, with my trunk packed and my name tapes sewn on by a woman in the village. The worst part was having to explain the cripple with the eye patch to the cruel, inquisitive girls who watched me arrive. I was not happy at boarding school. But I was even more unhappy when I came home.

My mother was recovering and had crawled back to claim her place as your wife and mother to your children. The babies hardly knew me. The bitter arguing, the territorial battles between mother and daughter began and the constant cry of "stop talking to Daddy" would pour from her lips as three years of only Daddy became a habit I could not break.

"Daddy, do you think?"

"Daddy, can I?"

"Daddy . . . Daddy . . . Daddy . . ."

"What about Mummy, for Christ's sake, what about Mummy?" she would scream.

A new era had dawned. I became a difficult, exhausting, troublesome girl and I heard their sighs of relief at the end of each school holiday.

chapter

19

I'm making rules Jack? I know, after the intense, sudden love that we have drowned in, I have to be cautious. I can't give myself back to you as I want to. I long to become a couple. But I know it wouldn't work. I know because it has happened before. Do you remember, could you forget?

When I married you I thought that all my problems would be over. I thought that this glorious man, who was so strong and loving, would change my life. Ah-ha, that was my first mistake. Now I've learned.

No one changes your life but yourself. We moved to Prestbury. To the mansion with eight bathrooms. A different pot to crap in each day, we laughed. The laughter halted. You crapped on me.

Working for Love

Within weeks the glowing, caring man I had clung to during our courtship became a moody, sulky tyrant. Every penny I spent had to be accounted for and written in a little book. I could not go out without your permission—if I did you became unbearably stroppy. Every evening you would return surrounded by an air of displeasure. Somehow my every move was incorrect. It was my fault. You were never there. Never there for me. You were driven, totally obsessed by your work. The novelty of me had worn off and a man compelled by his career appeared.

Because I had no friends I couldn't turn to anyone. A terrible spiral had begun. You at the controls and me becoming the controlled. It got to a stage when I would yearn for approval and still I couldn't do it right. I began to lose control and our nightly fights became physical. Not you against me but me against me. I would become so frustrated, so devastated at your never-ending irritation. At the silent disapproval and the complete emotional and financial control you had over me.

I would long to strike you, hurt you, kill you. But instead I would tear my arms to shreds with my nails, blood oozing from the paths of torn skin. I would batter my head against the wall and once, after a totally unreasonable accusation of a crime you had found me guilty of (without trial), I banged my hand against the wall and broke the bone.

Then I went to see your doctor. Begging for help. He sent me to see a psychiatrist. This eminent man, who had gone down the same road with your first

91

wife. Still he did not suggest that you see a psychiatrist. The psychiatrist never laughed, never smiled, and took notes all the time. I was convinced she was writing letters.

"What do you think?" I'd ask her.

"What do *you* think?" she'd reply.

Down into the depths of my childhood she would take me. Agonizing journeys, and just as we were (or at least I was) reaching a point so filled with pain, she would say, "I'm so sorry, but I'll have to stop you here."

And I would stumble down her stairway, my sobs accompanied by her white-noise machine.

Every week I would go and spill my childhood entrails and every week I would leave feeling worse.

"You have to reach the bottom. It is painful, but you must realize that once you have dealt with this you will come out a fuller person."

All week I had a man who blamed me. And then once a week I would pay a woman enormous sums of money to hear me recount my childhood of traumas.

It got to the stage where I couldn't drive the car, I was so disturbed when I left her office. So she started writing me prescriptions for Valium. Starting with 5 mg, then 10.

"They will make you shed the tears you should have shed for years," she said when I told her they made me depressed.

I couldn't get out of bed. I couldn't stop shaking. You began to sleep in the other room. I stopped eating.

Working for Love

Eventually my father persuaded you to bring me to London. They put me straight into hospital.

The psychiatrist who saw me wrote this letter to your learned doctor in Manchester:

> . . . She is beginning to find it difficult to communicate with her husband, at least partly because she relates to him as if he were a stern, disapproving, and exigent figure.
>
> Her current psychiatric management does not seem appropriate for two reasons. First—the administration of Valium is a short-term palliative that carries the risk both of inducing depression and of encouraging the view that Molly is disturbed, thereby invalidating her attempts to establish herself as a mature and responsible individual. Second—a psychotherapeutic approach which encourages Molly to reiterate traumatic events seems pointless since she has never repressed or failed to ventilate her anxieties and resentments about her father's attitude to the death of her sister, and his wish for Molly to act as a substitute for the dead child, her mother's illness, her father's private life, and her brother's incapacity. There is nothing to be gained by Molly going over this well-worn ground yet again to another interlocutor and the risk is she will be stuck in a posture of self-pity and childishness.
>
> I would recommend a practical approach aimed at strengthening her assets and enhancing her communication with her husband.

You agreed that we would start to work on our problems. You would start to treat me as an equal. Yes, you had been unkind. The psychiatrist in Manchester, realizing I was not going to return, started to panic and sent registered bills.

I've said, "I'm making the rules."

I've said, "I have to be cautious."

You know why, don't you Jack? Because this was not the only incident. This was not the only time an old dog learned new tricks, and then forgot them just as fast. This was not the sole incidence (leopards don't change their spots) of your total control games.

There was a wonderful lull of happiness and then back we went. So this time, I'm watching you, I'm sitting on the edge of the line just watching.

chapter
20

As adolescence took a total grip, we, as moody teenagers, assaulted our bodies horribly. We waged war against body hair, somehow thinking it would prolong our childhoods if it remained. Our legs became nursery slopes for razors. School baths would resemble abattoirs after shaving enormous slivers of skin as well as the fluffy, light-blond hairs my legs once grew. Creams, which we would smear in our armpits, stung and left rashes as we scraped at the little hairs with a spatula. Eyebrows plucked to arches, deodorant applied to every area imaginable (including behind our knees). We bought premoistened tissues for our vaginal areas and gazed at the chemist's shelves for even more products that could help us, hairless and sweet-smelling, on our way to womanhood. Periods were, of course, occasions of great joy and deep concern. Wads of sanitary ware to avoid leakage and the monthly paranoia of an "accident." Studying for our O levels, we reveled in the final throes of bodily changes.

I went home for the weekend before my O levels were due to start. Having never really worked at school I was dreading being caught out, as obviously the exam board would now do to me.

My mother (who had stunned the Western world with her virtual recovery) telephoned from America on Saturday at lunchtime and I heard my father protesting. "Rachel, you can't do this. She's about to take her O levels. No, absolutely not. Christ Rachel, this will not help, she'll never know normality if we do this."

I knew my escape route was in sight.

My father hung up and looked at me.

"It appears that there is an American director flying here as we speak. Mummy has suggested that he read you for the part of her daughter in the film she's about to make. I don't like it Molls, but she insists."

The American director appeared. He took me into the sitting room and for two hours made me read from his script and asked me very embarrassing questions about my sexual experiences.

I had had none, which seemed to delight him.

He left that afternoon and the next day we were in my headmistress's sitting room.

"Molly is hardly one of our scholarship girls so I think this will be harmless. After all, we know she plans to be an actress, so this is probably a beneficial exercise. However Molly, we wouldn't like to see you come back with a swollen head."

Daddy drove me to the airport. He mumbled a paragraph or two on "not dishing out sexual favors."

He had read the script; I had not.

"What's this girl like? This part I'm playing?" I asked him.

"She's very fey," he replied.

"Yes, this girl Fay," I said.

"Oh Molly, you are an ass, she's not called Fay." He sighed.

And so I left, not knowing the character's name, and not knowing what she was like, but I knew I was off on my own, ass or not.

Hello World. Hello Stardom. Hello, hello.

Good-bye O levels, good-bye—I'm about to become important.

I was important. For eight weeks I signed autographs, smiled at strangers who took my photograph. I had a chauffeur. I had a huge salary. I was a "natural," according to everyone involved. I was going to be a big star. I had an enormous hotel room. Oh yes, yes, yes, this was what I wanted my life to be. My mother sat back and watched it happen.

"They say I'm going to win an Oscar, Mummy."

"Well, isn't that nice, Molly," she'd reply.

There was one thing that troubled me. Not one man would look at me.

I was fifteen and nubile. Aching to experience sex. The whole film set and hotel was filled with young, able-bodied men. But they wouldn't acknowledge me. I used all my awkward teenage wiles, but to no avail.

We made the film. It was "hot," according to the people who knew. The dreaded day of flying back to England and school was looming. The eight solid weeks of attention were ending.

Panic started to fill me.

There was a boy, a boy I had ached for. A boy of eighteen who was to me a living god. He was beautiful. I had a crush, oh did I have a crush on him.

On my last night he came to my hotel room. I welcomed him. I was a woman, wasn't I? I was a movie star.

He got into my bed. An hour of immensely inexperienced groping took place. The sort of physical contact, rubbing, licking, rubbing again, that turns you red and leaves you confused. Then he left. I flew home. Filled with experiences to make my friends gasp. Within the next twelve months I discovered a number of confusing facts.

The first was that I was going to be a movie star and that meant I was beyond school. I was way past uniforms and bedtimes and work. And so I left. I simply ordered a taxi and left. My father laughed when I got home and my mother, realizing her folly, wept.

The next caused immense relief. In an interview I read with the director, he said that he had ordered the male population of the film unit not to go near me. I was virgin material and he wanted me to stay that way "for art's sake." What happened after the filming, he said, was "up to Molly."

I wrote a letter to my friend. My first bedmate. Telling him of my thrilling times. Telling him of my impending stardom and ceased education. I got the letter back stamped *Return to sender, addressee deceased.* He had gone with a gun to a field and shot himself.

The final discovery was simple. The film flopped. It opened and closed and no one knew. I did not win an Oscar.

So there I was. At home. Not quite sixteen. Not quite a woman. But I smelled nice and had no body hair. My one lover had killed himself, my one film had flopped, and my parents looked up at me and said, "Life's tough."

PART
TWO

chapter
21

My dearest Jack,

I know how aggressive and unpleasant this has become. I know it has gone over the edge. Too much anger is spewing out and it has gone too far. I am sure I am hell. I know I am hell. Shrouded in a wrapping of vast insecurity and confusion. Constantly dipping my toe into a pool of disharmony. Almost begging for drama. Longing to be the center of attention. Running to my father when we sway off course. Being a horribly disloyal wife and encouraging my family to mock you.

   I'm not denying any of my words to you. But it's time to grow up, isn't it? Perhaps you, at nearly fifty, and me at thirty, perhaps we've hurt each other enough.

I did it to my mother, too, you know. I was so terribly disloyal to her. I turn at the sound of my father's voice. Judas, what a Judas I am when he woos me. If he telephones me, I twitter. As do my sisters.

It's time to grow up. I said so at the start. I said it was time to stop pleasing you and Daddy and start pleasing myself. Okay, I'm doing that. It's time to start caring, it's time to start appreciating and stop hurting each other. Why have we all been manipulating each other for so many years?

I haven't written this for six weeks. I don't know why but I do know that I am glad we're back together. It's been a terribly difficult time, hasn't it? But oh my dear Jack, something amazing has happened to you.

Those first few weeks, when we started living together again. What a time of pain and total frustration. But I never stopped to think that perhaps you, too, were insecure. We kept falling into such desperate murky games. I'm not going into details, I've had enough of whining, but you know, don't you?

It seemed strange to me that the stronger and more self-assured I became, the more you tried to knock me off my perch. I had become the creature you had described to me. Your requirements of a perfect wife.

"I want someone who is strong, who can manage on her own and who needs me for loving and caring and not just to carry her through life."

It wasn't right though. When I reached my peak,
when I sold my first story to a women's magazine, my
euphoria was obliterated by your berating me all
evening.

It had got out of sight. I couldn't face another night
of spiraling and sparring. Some horrible destructive
force coming from both of us was relentless. I couldn't
take another night, another night of you in your pin-
striped suit and shining black shoes and me in my
designer clothes hurling abuse at each other again.
How could we have plummeted so far in such a short
time? Yet weren't we the new improved version? So
neatly repaired and polished up.

I walked out of the house. I got in the car and I
drove and I thought. At four A.M. I came home and I
tumbled into bed. The next day you got up, moody,
and didn't even say good-bye.

"Please come home, I have to talk to you."

"All right."

I stood against the banister, you sat glowering on
the bed. I knew it was a stab, a brave move, perhaps
mad? I knew if I said it wrong, it was curtains.

"I will never do it right for you Jack. I've just
realized that you are probably as insecure, or even
more so, than I am. You resent me and you resent my
family. As drawn to us as you are, you hate us."

You gazed at me, daring me to continue.

"You are a genius at business but you have nothing
else. No deep loves or passions. No stirring
involvements. Your children and your home are of
little interest to you, except as showcases. You have

no culture. Success ends at work. You know nothing about paintings, furniture, music, or wine. You have no interest in literature, and it makes you terribly insecure. I carry us through anything to do with people. I have brought you armfuls of life that you would never have known of if it wasn't for me. Yet I was always the one at fault and now I know why."

I stood, I stopped. You said nothing. This was the bravest I had ever been. Rubbish, this was the first time I had ever bothered to think of you.

For seven and a half years I had ceaselessly, donkey-like, carried my burdens, from country to country, simply accepting the blame, ultimately rearing up and kicking out at you, biting and braying. Not once had I settled down to consider what was going on in this man's head, this man I had married. This man I clearly loved. But why did I love him? To accept the blame was easy, to work out why I was being blamed was new to me.

I had run out on the battlefield, baring my chest, and had so amazed the enemy, so astounded the gunman that he sat paralyzed, wondering what I was going to do next.

"Now it seems simple. I married what I knew. I asked to be treated as a child and you were happy to treat me as such. You were also determined to keep me in that position. But once left on my own, once I realized I could survive very well, you got scared, and when I knew I was definitely doing what you told me to do and still in your eyes I was doing it wrong, then I realized. You need me more than I need you. I will never do it right, ever, because the only way you can retain your position of power is to keep pushing me down. The game is to keep me down. Criticize and control, as long as I am kept lower than you I will never rise to be your equal. Your greatest fear is that maybe I'll realize that I am stronger than you, more powerful than you, and could, maybe, be as successful. You cannot operate without a dependent partner. You resent me Jack, and you are dead scared of losing me.

"A master of manipulation, you pulled my strings for seven and a half years and as hard as you yanked, I was not moving in the right direction. This is it, I'm cutting the strings because it's time for the puppeteer to face the facts. He's as fucked up as his puppet."

Silence.

You stood up and walked toward me, an expression of emptiness on your face. It's a large room. I would guess it took twelve steps to reach me. During that time every possibility of your reaction flashed through my mind. You could walk right past me, down the stairs, and out of the door forever. You could get good and close and then snarl loathsome abuse in my face. You could wander over and wallop me. You could agree, but not totally—that would be unthinkable. Not the old Jack. The master of the slant of the head and quizzical expression. The crooked mouth that works in sync with a slightly puzzled frown that spells out misdemeanor. It would be impossible for this camel to give in.

One, two, three, four . . .

I leaned back in utter quiet.

Five, six, seven . . .

You walked forward, not giving me a hint.

Eight, nine, ten, eleven . . .

I think a smile started to travel across your lips.

Twelve.

"Molly, you're right. Everything you have just said is true. Totally true. I have never realized it until now. I am an unsteady, insecure man, who is desperately in love with you."

I was stunned.

"You are giving me an incredible break. I have never been able to admit to any of this stuff before. Perhaps I have never known it."

"Will you go and see a shrink?"

"Yes, yes I will."

I was in ecstasy.

"I'll do more than that. I'm going to start getting involved in the house. I'm going to start becoming a more interested father, and most of all, Molls, I'm going to stop trying to control you, and start loving you and giving you the attention you deserve."

chapter
22

I think we had all
reached a plateau. We had struggled up our hillsides
and were all having a bit of a picnic. This was no
feast, though, it was just a little snack that was leaving
each one of us unsatisfied and hungry.

By us I mean Mummy and Daddy and I. Not the
babies. They were living rather normal lives. Well,
normalish. Meriel was saving all her money for a sex
change in Tunisia, Mathew was struggling with a tu-
tor, and Fanny was a baby giraffe. Long legs, a giggly
head, and terribly pretty.

The three of us, survivors but clearly needing.
Daddy should have been content. He had become an
enormously successful, wealthy, and famous man. It

was as if Mummy, being incapacitated, had forced him into reaching his massive potential. He had become a star and was enjoying it. He had lived as my mother's shadow for twenty years. Perhaps he was almost overenjoying it?

Yet his male ego, which had for all those years been forced to lie dormant, was now becoming insatiable.

My mother was doing her best. She was a living legend. The first victim of such immense brain damage ever to recover. The frustration she felt with herself came out in spurts of fiery temper. To have been as famous and independently ravishing as she for forty years and then kiss it good-bye is terribly difficult. She limped, she had trouble with her memory, and she was ravaged. The most exhausting thing for her was the newfound love for her husband. The Svengali who had brought her back from the dead. There was a dependence.

And we needed. Mummy and I. Like two baby birds in a nest squawking for food, we sat open-beaked, craving his attention. He had total control now. Not only financially, but he had also taken over the running of the house. I don't know how it happened but it did. Things Mummy was struggling to run. It's strange, really, because he rehabilitated her, it was he who wanted to rebuild his wife, yet just as she was about to add the final touches, toddlerlike he knocked the sand castle down.

I'm the king of the castle.

"I'm leaving it all up to Papa now," she would say with resignation.

It was easier for her, and his constant meddling and complaining were wearing her down.

She didn't give up at once. They had horrific clashes for a while. Martinis and wine had become a prop and from about seven o'clock the battles would rage.

"You make me so furious Papa. It's my goddamn house but you've taken it over."

"Christ Rachel, I'm running four children, sorting out their lives, schools, and bullshit. I'm taking care of you and your career. I'm paying massive bills. You bloody actresses, selfish women. You need to work, then you'll be happy."

He would push her to do jobs.

"I don't want to go away for eight weeks Papa."

"Yes you do. When you get there you'll love it and everyone will love you."

"If you say so."

It was easier without her; she had become so demanding.

So she'd go, and he'd run the house and when she returned she had less of a grasp of it all. Home, children, staff, friends. I became his ally. She was clearly driving him mad, I understood. I didn't really have anywhere else to go. I wasn't qualified to do a job. So I stayed at home.

The only thing I had any interest in was caring for my man. I wasn't very good at anything else. Mistresslike I would long for Mummy to go so I had him to myself. Yet once she was gone he took very little notice of me. He went up to London most nights to

111

gamble at his club and during the day he worked. We never talked. We never, ever discussed our feelings or thoughts. I could sense a deep unhappiness growing within. Yet, as I had tuned in to him through feigned misery after Mary's death, the only way I could now tune in was by sharing and agreeing with his growing loathing of Mummy. I didn't need to be persuaded. Oh Daddy, I'm here. I'm all yours. Together we will cope with our exhausting brood.

He instilled in me a belief that Mummy was a terrible burden and he had to endure her with silent suffering. We began to treat her with a certain humorous disdain. While she, actress that she was, played up to us.

Even when she returned from working she would detach herself from the household. She would limp down to the village with a basket and pick up the rubbish people had littered the street with. She would wander around the garden pulling up weeds and cutting the roses.

"I'm only good for trash and suckers," she'd say.

As a child who dares his parents to challenge him and misbehaves in order for them to prove their love, so did she. And he looked more and more exhausted and she became bitter. Their drinking was excessive and never did a night pass without a massive explosion of frustration.

And I watched helpless and keen.

Keen to wipe up the wine when he smashed the bottle on the floor because she wouldn't stop arguing. Keen to make him a little light supper when she went off to play bridge. Keen to lock up the house because he'd gone to bed in a sulk and she had staggered off to another room in a rage.

But they missed so much of me. They missed my little jokes. They missed the stories I would tell Meriel and Fanny at bedtime. They missed my sobbing when the dog would go missing and I would search all night in the fields and woods, for he was the only one who ran away when they started to scream. They also missed my rather blatant whimper for help, until, on my seventeenth birthday, I had not eaten a meal for three weeks and collapsed as I cooked them breakfast.

chapter
23

Oh Jack, Jack, Jack, Jack, Jack. What a state of
euphoria am I in. Isn't it incredible that we can be so
happy and as one?

Let's have another baby, Jack. Now we know how
much we love each other. Now we are behaving as
adults.

I feel so deeply immersed in love for you. I cannot
believe the pain that we have put each other through
when we can share such joy. And you come home
from work, not with a sigh and a long jaw, but like a
husband in a coffee commercial with a satisfied smile
and aura of total happiness. I will nurture you, for I
have so much to give and now you are here for me to
give it. In the past, even when you were physically

present you did not communicate with me. Well, you did in our early days but certainly not lately. Yet here we are sharing and I feel such contentment. Never in my whole life have I been treated as an equal and here we are. It doesn't hurt, does it? My giant, my overachiever, see, you don't have to carry us all by yourself. I can easily manage half. I could manage it all if I had to.

I feel well. I do not need to be on an operating table to catch you as you dash past, briefcase in hand. I can make a suggestion without your feeling threatened. I do not feel as if I faked my credentials and betrayed you into marrying me. I am your wife and you think I am a hot ticket and oh, how I respond.

I went to see Barry the shrink today. I filled him to the brim with my ecstasy and he looked back at me and said, "Just remember Molls, old dogs don't learn new tricks this easily. I hate to sound cynical, but I don't want you to fall too far, if, of course, you fall at all."

But this old dog is special and I shall brush him and feed him and have total faith in him. Because without faith he'll slink away again.

And just for the record, this old dog bought two plants from an unemployed teenager at the door today.

chapter
24

I was not a particularly effective anorexic. I didn't play the part very well. As soon as my parents had turned around and noticed, I thought it was all all right. For a brief moment I was the center of attention. It was lovely. I had another car journey alone with Daddy. The smell of tobacco and leather. The comfort of his Rover seats that gently embraced. The intimacy of an hour in the car, just for me, a drama for me. And I would pour his coffee from his thermos. We did not talk. The radio would play classical music as it did when he drove Mummy.

"For Christ's sake, turn that radio off and talk to me," she used to nag.

Not me. I knew he would not talk. It was enough that he was present, driving me, specially. I had never known the thrill before of being the center of a drama. Things had been pretty quiet on the tragedy side of our lives and in looking back I know that they were glad to have my starvation as a diversion. Buzzing with new drama, it was just like old times. He drove me all the way to the doctor's and came in.

Oh, great controller, didn't we do well? Together, but with you leading, yet without any prior plan. Tumbling words came spouting out, blaming Mummy. The two of us totally in tune. We painted a picture of this heartless, selfish star, a terrible unfeeling woman; the blame was easily hers.

I watched and listened, nodding heartily while you told of the burden of running the household, earning the money, and my mother's inadequacy.

Did we ever discuss it? Had we ever once actually been open and had a conversation. Oh no. There was nothing wrong with you Dad, it was all her.

The doctor, he was happy to leave this pile of familial vomit as it was and prescribed mood-altering pills for me. Clearly he was content to take the word of the great man and bill-payer at face value. "Clearly what Molls needs is a proper mother," he said.

We drove home and entered a new era.

Daddy was so kind to me. So loving, or at least attentive. He used to go out and buy me special foods to lure me to eat and I would make him happy by sitting beside him and finishing every little bit. We still didn't talk but I knew I was noticed.

117

It was such a time of closeness. Mummy was away and together we ran our busy home.

I didn't need a proper mother.

So why? Why Daddy, wasn't I enough?

I denied it for over a year. I didn't see it for over a year. I wouldn't, I couldn't.

You were so good during that period Daddy; I was so good. You didn't have to take the doctor's advice quite so literally. "Clearly what Molls needs is a proper mother."

But then you always had to have someone else to blame, didn't you?

chapter
25

I lay in bed last night Jack, and for the first time in my
life I was aware of an inner peace. A sudden
knowledge had overtaken my soul. I felt a calm I had
never felt before. I knew I was in a situation that I
could cope with and accept. Where were you? Who
was lying beside me? It wasn't the long, warm body I
had become so used to. It didn't have the glowing,
hairy surface I've touched a thousand times. Not the
straight back covered in brown spots like a speckled
egg. Not the dampness of your nighttime heat. It was
not you. Close to me, touching for reassurance, crying
out in pain, whimpering in confusion. It was not your
vomit I had spread towels over throughout the night,

with each throw-up upon the bottom sheet. It was
your baby son.

Never have I been so alone. Just me, Gwennie, and
Sam. For two days he had been so ill and I had
telephoned the doctor, who dismissed it as "a little
bug." It was a weekend. Friday night he was awake all
night while I rocked him. When I tried to give him the
Paracetemol he struggled and knocked the spoon out
of my hands. Eventually, covered in pink slime, I tied
his arms down with a muslin nappy. He needed to be
held and rocked and the few times I put him down I
would carry on rocking to and fro. He screamed for
attention and comfort if he was not in my arms. The
stove felt cooler than him when I boiled the kettle.

Gwennie would wake and say, "Baby Sam not
well."

"No darling, he's not."

We were all in my bed. Just as I had calmed him
down he would sit bolt upright, eyes wide, and throw
up all over us.

My father always told me never, ever to call the
doctor on a weekend. So after my initial call, I tried to
cope alone. I did eventually call on Sunday night and
once again I allowed myself to be dismissed as
overreacting.

While Sam, my little baby Sam was tossing and
writhing. And we were alone. At one point I cut my
hand, in the little flappy bit between fingers and it
bled, bled a lot. I walked around the house with baby
Sam tossing his head backward and forward, crying
such a disjointed, pained noise, with my right hand

held high in the air to try and stop the blood from
pouring out.

Little Gwennie tagging around behind us, aware that
she must take second place. My mother's help, Helen,
had taken Daisy on holiday to Scotland.

And then last night, when little Sam was so ill, far
iller than before. Hotter and limp. Once lulled into a
brief sleep, that was when it happened. Gwennie was
curled up at the edge of the bed, Sam was lying on
my chest, moaning in his sleep. I just felt a wave pass
over me. A newfound calm, a knowledge I had never
had before. "I'm on my own, I'm faced with things I
have always feared and I can cope. I'm frightened. I
think my baby is dying but I will manage. My husband
is missing and I will be all right."

Where were you Jack? I did not know. You had
gone on a sailing holiday with your friends to the
Greek islands.

"I love you Molly and I don't want to go."

"But darling you must. It just seems such a waste,
such a waste of a holiday, time we could be spending
together."

You had to go, you said. On this sailing trip you had
planned when we were apart. A silly sort of
retribution trip. I knew you had arranged it to show
me that you could go off and have fun. Since then we
had reunited and suddenly you didn't want to go. We
had breakfasted together before you left for the
airport.

"Where are you staying?" I asked.

"I don't know, Molly."

"Please Jack, please, please will you call me and tell me where you'll be and how I can reach you? So often in the past you've gone on trips and not bothered to let us know where you are."

"Of course I will Molly, I'll call you tonight."

We walked toward the taxi; you were crying.

"Molly, I'm really going to miss you, I'm sorry I'm leaving."

"It seems a pity, when we haven't had a holiday for two years, but perhaps you need to go and prove that you can have fun without me."

"I'll call you tonight."

"Good-bye darling, I'll be in, waiting."

That was five days ago. Your office called yesterday and left a number where I could "reach you." All the while Sam was vomiting and crying last night, I was dialing this number, somewhere in the Mediterranean, that rang and rang and was never answered.

Now today I am in a children's hospital in London. My son, your son is unconscious, IV in his fragile wrist. By the time I arrived at the doctor's in London his temperature was 105.

His nappy was filled with blood this morning and when we arrived at the hospital he threw up; he threw up such a horrific substance and I said to the nurse, "What's that?"

Never had I seen anything so horrid, so distressing, for both him and me.

"Bowel matter," she answered while she sponged him down.

I had telephoned a friend and asked her to hold

him in the car this morning. It was seven-thirty and he
was semiconscious. We went to the country doctor
who said, "I can see he's a very sick baby, but I'm
terribly busy, so bring him back this afternoon and I'll
review the situation."

I showed him the blood-filled nappy.

"I'll ask you to take that home with you."

His look of disgust, so evident. How could a man, a
person so entrusted to care for my baby, be so
precious, so busy, so uninvolved?

I wrapped the blood-filled nappy back in the silver
foil I had brought it in.

"But he's not usually like this, Dr. Matheson. Look
at his eyes."

"He's not having a fit, if that's what you are
worried about."

"Of course I know that."

I picked up the foil package, wrapped Sam in his
blanket, collected Gwennie and my friend on my way
through the waiting room. We drove to London in
silence. Every ten minutes or so I would say, "Is he
still breathing?"

"Yes, he is," she would answer.

When our pediatrician in London took us through to
his room the dam burst in my chest. Tears started to
well up in my eyes; at last there was someone to care
and help me.

We were rushed to hospital. There he lies, my little
hollow baby. Moaning softly, so white and fragile in
his metal cot.

Your son is lying between bars unconscious.
Wouldn't you like to know, Jack?

But I don't need you. I discovered I can cope. The
two things I have always feared have happened to me
this year and I paced myself through them. My
husband left me and my baby has nearly died. Alone,
I dealt with them. I didn't generate any of my old
drama-filled games, I told no one except people who
needed to know for practical reasons. I stretched
myself without stretching others. I bent without
breaking.

And we'll make it, Daisy, Gwennie, Sam, and I.

But will you?

You are missing. Missing so much, so much of us.
How could you let it spoil so quickly?

I have just tried that number again; there was an
answer.

"I wonder if I could speak to Jack Scott, please?"

"He's not here madam."

"But is he staying there?"

"Oh no madam, this is not a hotel, this is a
marina."

"So where is he staying?"

"I think he is staying at the Lindos Bay Hotel."

"Are you sure?" I gulped.

"Pretty sure."

"All right, well, when you see him could you ask
him to call this number please and speak to his wife?"

"Yes, I will madam. Good-bye."

You are staying at Lindos Bay. You are staying at

WORKING FOR LOVE

Lindos Bay. I cannot comprehend this total betrayal.
Lindos Bay on Rhodes, where we were meant to have
our holiday this year, the one you canceled. So what
did you do? Did you just tell them to hang on to the
deposit? Did you know all along that you were going
there? The hotel that we chose together, with such
care and thought. I am tired Jack, I feel so tired. I
have been awake for the last three nights with Sam. I
was okay, but now, but now I feel worn out. While I
could have slept, a little phone at the end of the pier
somewhere in the Mediterranean was ringing
pointlessly, ring, ring, ring, ring.

chapter
26

Western met Grace on an autumn evening. Daddy said she would be a perfect match for a film director he and Mummy were wooing. Or was the director wooing them? Or was everyone wooing each other? Yes, that's right, they were.

He had met her in California, he said, at the Beverly Hills Hotel. She was an American divorcée about to move to London, an "interior decorator." Mummy cooked, which was, by then, a rarity. Prawns in Paradise and Chicken Tarragon, then Almond Whirl. She had a subconscious territorial instinct that night. It was almost like the old Mummy; she rallied herself, serving the food, cracking jokes, and looking radiant.

Her swan song.

Dad in Paradise.

We had a good time. All of us. We all liked Grace. Mum, me, Dad, and the film director.

A friendship started to blossom. Actually, a number of friendships started to blossom and Grace, clever Grace, cultivated us all. One by one. She was in the process of establishing herself in England. Her apartment was staggeringly elegant and we each saw it in turn and quite separately. It was all individual attention. Like a watchmaker, she had realized that we were delicate little cogs that operated independently yet in sync with each other. Performing our own little jobs but always rubbing the next little cog. And that without the constant friction we could not function at all. She also recognized the roles of each of us and the dust, grime, and grit that were sticking us together and causing us to malfunction; she saw that too.

Our saving Grace. How she befriended us that winter.

To Mummy she was an intimate girlfriend. She really seemed to like her. Poor Mummy didn't have any girlfriends by then and was delighted by Grace. Together they would go shopping, have lunches, and exchange secrets. Mummy would return from her outings with Grace, bags brimming. Lampshades, nighties, and newfound knowledge.

"Grace thinks I should have a face-lift. She thinks it will be really good for me."

"You know, that's a hell of a good idea," said Dad.

Mummy had her face-lift. It went very wrong. She

was a heavy smoker and coughed so much that the stitches split as she was coming around. She had to stay in hospital for a long time. Well, that wasn't Grace's fault. It was nice for Daddy, though, because he would often meet Grace in Mummy's hospital room and together they could go out for supper. He always asked Mummy first and she was happy to agree. It was rare for Daddy to like a friend of Mummy's. Anyway, it all made sense because Grace was dating the film director, who was away a lot, and he was a friend of Daddy's. And I, I had found the mother I'd yearned for. To be like Grace. To have her style, her class, her knowledge of all things.

She would let me confide in her, matters I could never share with anyone else. It was she who helped me find my first flat in London and my first job.

"You really need to get away from home Molls. It's simply unacceptable that you stay."

We never questioned her decisions. She had such conviction, such a possession of herself and all around her.

I would be invited to her flat for supper about once a week.

Always just the two of us, girls together. I would breathe her air. Run my finger along her desk, gaze awesomely at her invitations (she even knew royalty), and long to tell her new secrets.

With her you would divulge it all, the words would rush out, gush out, tumble and spill. She had a gift for milking people and you would want to tell it. Deepest, darkest stuff, and she would understand.

When Mummy came out of hospital, Grace came home and nursed her for a month.

When Grace had her tonsils out, she came home and Mummy nursed her for a month. Grace was not a good patient. She cried a lot, an awful lot.

She hunted out the nanny her children had had and passed her on to us. A tough old bird, not what Mathew, Fanny, and Meriel were used to. You see, Grace had left her husband when her children were very young.

As bread needs yeast to make it swell and grow, so we needed Grace. She had arrived at a perfect time, we were flat and soft and she molded us. When I heard that Daddy had canceled our usual holiday to Italy and had booked a farmhouse in France, I was delighted. Grace was holidaying with her children in the same village. What a change it would make from the predictable Positano. Whining Fanny and Meriel under the wisteria. Moaning Mummy as we dragged her up the steps. Calamari, move aside, it's foie gras time.

France was a vast success. For the first time in my memory everyone was happy. It was the sort of holiday I imagined other people at school used to have. I had always wanted to be like other girls at school.

The mothers who sent Valentine cards and Advent calendars. We never had normality. Mummy never knew how to do it properly. But now we had Grace to guide us all.

That was the holiday Mummy was hot. Photographs in the album record it. I'm not romanticizing or overdramatizing. There are pictures taken by Daddy of her and she has a coquettish look, a sexuality dredged up by the salvage man.

She was clearly feeling needed and wanted and how she blossomed. The twinkle through the lens at the man pressing the button.

Daddy, too, was a sunbeam. Like an excited teenager. He sparkled, he cracked terribly funny jokes, and he seemed to listen to us all, without the haunted, empty gaze and resigned replies.

Blissful summer, summer of terraces and barbecues, of champagne and vines.

Grace had resurrected us.

That autumn we had a first-anniversary dinner to celebrate our year-forged friendship.

I was living in London permanently. It had happened with such skillful planning that I had felt no pain.

Grace simply hatched a plot with me to persuade Dad to buy me a flat in the next street to hers. Within months I was ensconced in a very comfortable little apartment. The paternal umbilical cord was cut and stitched and tucked away neatly.

For the winter I took a job, working as a receptionist at a commercial company, friends of Grace's.

I started to spread my need to nurture; with it I spread my legs. Robbed of my little brood at home. No Daddy to purr and curl around. Not so easy. Not so safe. Gentlemen came and went. The sex was pointless and emotionally painful. This was the permissive era. We were all fucking. Magazines were

telling us how to have multiple orgasms with men
met in bars. While I struggled to discover orgasm
singular. A quest for love became a search for physical satisfaction. But oh, how I satisfied these men. As
they heaved themselves on top of me and pumped
away, I would curl my long legs around their necks
and give and give and give. Walruslike they rolled off,
having snorted, nostrils flared like bulls', and ejacu-
lated. Then they would flake out. While I lay wide-
awake, gazing at the Laura Ashley walls and curtains,
sticky-thighed. I was an immoral, stupid, empty girl.
But no one minded. No one ever bothered to say,
"Hang on Molls, it takes a lot of time and trust to fill a
void."

So the void got bigger. With every ended affair.
Let's not get too prim about this. Some of these guys
were one-night stands. But I didn't want them to be.
Oh no, I wanted each of them to be my husband,
each one in turn. Oh, how I could have loved them
all. I was honored to be in their arms. Silly Putty,
that's what I was. You could bounce me, mold me,
then crush me with your palm and bounce me again.

I told Grace, I shared all my secrets with her.

"You really need to find a man, a substitute for your
father," she said.

The search continued.

Blinded by my own inadequacy. Convinced I was
not worthy of love, delighted when this was once
again disproven by another man willing to bed me.

I bought *Bride's* magazine and yearned.

I knew it would all be all right once I had a man to

call my own. I still had Daddy, my weekend lover, to nurture and care for. Yet Grace was there, too, now. Every weekend, and as much as I loved her, I felt a twinge of resentment when she made him laugh. Mummy was away for three months that summer. The summer I met Peter. I was ripe, as ripe as the plums in the orchard. Daddy would hold the ladder while I climbed up and picked them.

"Yikes, there's a wasp."

"Don't be an ass Molly, just pick them."

Grace wasn't frightened of the wasps. We made plum compote and served it the night Peter came for supper. Peter, Peter, friend of Grace's. Peter the writer. Peter. I gazed at you over my glass of wine and laughed. Oh, how I laughed. Sharp, witty, and precise. Later that night when they had all gone to bed, we sat and talked. What a man, such direction. So right, so sure. He leaned over me and said, "Let's go to bed."

"I can't possibly do that, I've only just met you."

"Oh for Christ's sake don't be so middle class."

We soared, we tumbled, and we moaned.

Then Peter started to tell me. He could show me, teach me, mold me. I was doing it all wrong, even kissing, even kissing badly. But he would redeem me. Didn't I see, didn't I see?

I see, Peter, I see, I'm ready. Oh yes, this is just like old times.

chapter
27

You were so damn beautiful, unshaven and rugged. I
could have allowed you to pick me up, Rhett
Butleresque, while I lay limp in your arms. Those days
are over, though. Anyway, the Portland Hospital for
Children is not a fitting place for King Kong poses.
This time it was I holding limp little Sam. You had a
very defensive shine in your eyes.

"You've got a great tan," I said.

"It was hot."

I bet it was.

"You know, I'm not sure why you came back."

"I wanted to help."

"It's too late Jack. I needed your help last week.
While I was alone at home. I've needed your help for

the last seven and a half years. If I think of all the times I've begged you to join us, to be a part of us—not some demigod gazing at us from a distance, occasionally showing your approval when we make a sacrificial gesture. I can't hack it. You'll never apply yourself.

"But if you really love, you know, if you genuinely love—proper love not ownership love—you do something about it, and you do it as very best you can. Even if it means learning, forsaking, or accepting. It's all a commitment and you were never willing to totally commit."

"Yes, I was."

"No you weren't. Oh yes, you could commit for a few days, even a week, but never longer. You wouldn't apply yourself, not to an equal partnership. It's a game to you. Like some people have hobbies to distract their minds and do after work. We were your hobby, a game and a rather cruel game, for you to play when it suited you."

"I'm going to change, Molly."

"No you're not, and I now know I can't change you. This week I discovered something. I discovered I don't need a husband, I don't need an owner, a lord and master. I need a partner, I need a friend."

"I've been an ass, I'll be your friend."

I gazed at Sam. Oblivious Sam, asleep in my arms. I've often marveled at Sam's calm. If I consider the trauma and sadness I experienced during my pregnancy with Sam. Because I knew, deep down and

swelling daily as my belly swelled, I knew that Jack
was getting bored with us.

As if he had been immunized in utero, as if such a
vast dose of misery had been injected into him and he
had developed the antibodies, my little Sam was filled
with peace. As this agonizing exchange, this gut-
ripping, body-sizzling conversation was passing
through his airwaves, he slept. Still I rocked to and
fro.

"But can you? I don't believe you can. One visit to
the shrink Jack, and you gave up. Two attempts at
coming home in time to see the kids before they went
to bed and then you stopped. I am fed up with false
starts, I'm fed up with begging, asking, wanting you to
be the person I thought you were. Longing to be
spoken to, longing to be taken notice of. Having to
create a drama to grab your attention. If I think of our
most intimate moments they've been centered around
disasters. Hospital bedsides, operations, and now, ill
babies. Why can't we be together at a family meal? A
picnic, you know, just normality? Why does it have to
be a scream before you notice? I'm so tired, I'm so
tired of being a chameleon, changing colors all the
time to protect myself from the predator. I've been
trying to be someone else all my life, I've been
apologizing, adapting, turning into other people's
needs for nearly all my life, in order to be loved. I'm
tired of this play. I've always been the understudy."

"I won't do it anymore, I'll be your ally; let me be
your partner."

It's eight P.M. My partner has gone out to buy Big

Macs. I'm giving it one more chance. I want to be married. Because I believe in marriage, I got married for good. I will work and work and not give up. I have put so much, invested such love, such sadness, such care, such time in this family. The years of begging, pleading for notice. Please God, tell me they are not in vain. I have a brood, I have children, I cannot allow seven and a half years of hard work, pure, draining effort to be wasted. While he, surely he knows how important this union is? How vital his cog is to our machinery.

Why do I keep hearing terrible things? I have earache, I don't like to listen, it hurts. You are being disloyal to me Jack. Totally destructive and cruel. Perpetuating a feeling. An aura of self-pity hangs around you. People who mean a lot to me, each one in turn you work on and delicately spoon little stories about me into them. Untrue stories, tales of woe for Jack. My stepmother, my father, my aunt, my best friend. So the wheel turns slowly and I am strapped upon it as your burden, poor old Jack, what he has to put up with. Even shopkeepers. I was out yesterday and I went to collect a dress I had ordered. The assistant started hesitantly and then gushed into full flow.

"I hope you don't mind me telling you this, but I feel you should know—I've always believed in sisterhood and all that. Please don't repeat it but when your husband came in the other day to look at the things you'd chosen for your birthday, he was so rude about you. I mean really horrid and he, well, he had

someone with him, actually, and he was telling her
something about you, which we could all hear."

"What?"

"Oh God, I know I shouldn't be telling you this, but
you're such an old customer I feel like you're a friend.
It was some stupid story about the weekend and how
you'd insisted on his coming with you to some fund-
raising dinner he hadn't even been told about. How
he had been playing squash with your sister and then
visited your parents and at eight you'd telephoned and
started screaming at him because he wasn't home,
and ready to go out."

Okay Jack, you bastard. You know I asked you ten
days ago if we could go, as I had been asked as guest
of honor to an important charity dinner. At six forty-
five you informed me that you would be playing
squash and hoped to be back by eight. I pleaded with
you not to go, "you know I said we have to be there
by eight."

"Okay Molly, I'll be back in time," you snapped.

Well, you weren't and I had to call around. I found
you at my father's house.

"Having a quick Scotch, why don't you pop down
with my suit and I'll shower and change here?" you
suggested.

"But Jack, we're meant to be there now, you knew
that."

"Listen Molly, don't start being difficult."

I knew, and you knew, my parents were listening.

"Forget it Jack, I'll go alone."

You hung up and turned to my parents and said, "I

137

don't know how I manage. She sprang this on me tonight and now she's screaming at me. I suppose I'll have to go to keep her happy."

My stepmother was impressed by your thoughtfulness and lent you some of Daddy's clothes to wear. You arrived halfway through dinner, hangdog.

That's right Jack, keep up the good work. Loony, nutty, demanding Molly. Irrational, complaining Molly.

I keep hearing, Jack, it all gets back to me. Why, why does an important man like you, a man of vast intelligence and power, need to make up stories about his wife? Fabrications in order to increase his martyrdom and her inadequacies. More and more I hear them. To my family and friends, and they all believe you, Jack. I feel like a doctor's wife who cannot go and complain that her husband is battering her. But Jack, surely you don't need to elevate your sense of suffering to encompass my shopkeepers?

Surely the game you are playing at home is enough.

chapter
28

*V*ulnerable in Latin is
translated as "capable of being wounded." Which I
was. The word *vulnerable* implies misguided trust. I
trusted totally, I have always totally trusted and plan
to continue doing so.

Thus, I was vulnerable, I was open—I still am.
Completely open and honest. I do wish the people
around me had been more honest and open. It would
have made the journey much easier for us all. Honest
with themselves, not simply with others.

Mummy had gone away to work for ten weeks. I
had let my flat and come home to take care of Daddy.
I have always called it home, I probably still will at
eighty. Dad was going up to London to gamble. He

seemed keen for me to have "a good night's sleep," which was a mystery to me—I generally did sleep well. He came downstairs in his suit, ready to leave, and just as he was pouring himself a drink (he used to drink in the car) and I was leaning against the fridge watching this wonderful monument, all six foot six, carrying out a regular ritual (so comfortable we were, so familiar was this home), he said, his back still facing me, "Molls, I've got these wonderful new sleeping pills. They really are marvelous, I thought you could try one tonight and have a good, sound sleep."

I've always had a penchant for pills, we were raised on rattling bottles.

"Okay Dad, why not?"

He had the pill, already in his pocket, he turned around and handed it to me and lolloped off to tickle the tables.

I watched telly and chatted to the cook. Meriel, Fanny, and Mathew were all away at school.

Hot milk has always been so cozy and at ten I took my mug up to bed and swallowed the "marvelous" pill with the first gulp. I even remember what I was reading. *Brideshead Revisited.* Peter had been insisting I become more literate. He used to test me on books.

"Who wrote *Catcher in the Rye*?"

"What was Lillian Hellman's first play?"

"I don't know, Peter."

"Well, you damn well should."

I was working on it.

Brideshead is the sort of book that makes you feel

as if you have a new set of friends. Well, I certainly needed them that night. I turned off the light at about ten forty-five and went to sleep.

I was woken by his car at one A.M. I can forever remember the sound of the big wheels crunching on the drive, the stopping, then the hum of reversing into the garage. Garage doors shutting, step, step down the path to the front door, the key turned. It was all so totally comforting, noises of childhood, predictable, mixed with the fuzziness of the sleeping pill. I knew what he would do next. I was secure in my knowledge. He would let the dogs out, they would bark, then he would give them their biscuits, put them to bed, turn on the burglar alarm, and come upstairs and go to bed himself.

I heard the barking, I heard the biscuit tin rattle, the mosquito hum of the alarm as he hoiked himself up the stairs, down the corridor, and into his room. I waited for him to lollop into his bathroom, but no, he moved with a purpose. I could hear his stride, he had direction, he went to his dressing room, then about-turned and went down the stairs.

Confusion and an overwhelming sense of foreboding pulled me out of my bed and to the banister. I heard him pick up the telephone and dial.

My heart was pumping; I prayed, "Please God, please God, he is calling Mummy, isn't he?"

These were the stairs, these stairs that allowed the ambulance men to rush my darling Mary down. It was exactly the same spot, the same warm wall that I pressed myself against when I watched totally bewil-

141

dered as they took Mary away. The same panic was beginning to overcome me, that all too familiar siren was echoing in my instinctive gut. I knew at the point Daddy, my Daddy, started to speak, that something horrible was happening.

"Madame Hynes, *s'il vous plaît.*"

I also knew that I was eavesdropping, an all too familiar pose. These stairs had been host to my little body swathed in white Victorian nightie when I was trying to comprehend Mary's death. The sleeping pill did not do me any favors. Why couldn't I be asleep? Why was I hearing this appalling, erotic conversation? How could Daddy be saying these things, the voice of passion. A tone of total love, his complete betrayal, his oblivion to all life but this telephone at the bottom of the stairs.

As a rabbit freezes when faced by car headlights, I froze. Not daring to move, yet totally aware I was about to fall into a well so dark and deep that I might never find a foothold and pull myself out.

They continued as I listened.

Nausea started to overwhelm me and a deep mist was beginning to settle over my body. A mist of dull gray, a fog of misery. His conversation continued. It was utterly horrible. The reality of my father carrying on in this totally amorous vein was appalling. I knew, I knew then what I had really known for the last two years. Daddy, my Daddy, was in love with Grace. Our Grace. He was more in love with her than any of us. He was saying things to her that he would never, ever have said to my mother or to me. I knew this man, I truly knew him, but who was this Lothario downstairs, this gentle, soothing, cooing lover?

I realized that he was about to hang up; somehow my legs took control and got me into bed. There I lay. I heard him come upstairs. I heard all the old familiar sounds. The thudding shoes as he threw them down in relief, having bent his old, tired body over his long, long legs to reach them.

The swishing and gurgling in the bathroom, the heaving into bed with a sigh. I heard all this as I lay. I did not feel the warmth of the familiarity. I did not listen with a secure knowledge, not now.

My entire body and soul was being devoured by a new demon. A great destructive force had swirled its way into our safe house and I lay still, knowing it would reach us all, and that lying in bed playing dead was not going to make it go away.

chapter
29

Marathon dancers in the thirties, that's what we are
like Jack. We started with verve and enthusiasm, you
leading and me happy to be swayed in your arms.
Blind to the grueling times ahead, we spun around.
When I trod on your toes, I said sorry; when you trod
on mine, I said sorry too. The whirling turned to
quickstep and each new move you wanted me to
perform was more complicated and difficult than the
last. Then I started to become exhausted—my arms
wrapped tightly around your neck; you supported me
around the floor until I was totally wiped out and
completely dependent on your strength.

A rest would leave us both refreshed and we'd go
back with renewed enthusiasm, tiring more quickly

each time. You lacked staying power; I would have carried on and indeed started to lead when you faltered. But what a couple, never quite in step, always swirling, tiring, and yet never completely stopping. And each rest would bring new resolutions, plans, and promises. But we hadn't remembered how quickly we tired last time, had we? Or learned the old steps properly.

Why do we keep it up? Is it the prize money? Oh no, it's not that. Is it the need to prove ourselves, maybe? Or is it the adrenaline that pumps when we get back on the dance floor? I am frightened of failure, I am so frightened of failure. But is it a failure when you have worked as hard as I have to make a good marriage? Is it a failure if I've tried, truly tried? I found all the letters I'd written to you over the last seven and a half years Jack. So sad, such sad, pleading letters. They all said the same thing, they all begged but the tone changed even though the message didn't.

In the early days of our marriage I was filled with apologies.

"I know I'm awful and neurotic and don't deserve your love, but please take some notice of me, please try and accept me—you don't have to understand me but you could talk to me."

Up until now.

"I am your equal, I am not a child, I deserve to be treated as your partner and not as a liability. Stop using expressions like 'I have to learn how to deal with you.' "

You make the rules—there are no rules. You do not deal with your wife; you share and respect.

But Jack, you couldn't share or respect. Because you would never open wide enough to acknowledge me as a grown-up. You married a child and a free spirit and you made it your life's work to break that spirit. I became a grown-up for you, I wore silk dresses and went to the hairdresser's twice a week, but I mislaid a part of me along the way and I did it for you.

There are two things I want you to think about, think long and hard. Things I have known about you. Maybe it was different before, but with me, these things are relevant.

The first is simple: You have never been upset emotionally. Angry yes, but upset, sad, hurt, pained— no. You will cause immense unhappiness in your mate then accept no responsibility for it. You do not seem to suffer at all.

The second is: What are you denying?

Why won't you go and talk to a therapist? Why do you think you are so spotless and that I must keep working on myself?

"There's nothing wrong with me darling."

That's what you said. But Jack, you won't face up to anything. You have to control it or walk away. Your mind is like a series of passages and if you don't like what's happening in one corridor, you will walk away and shut the door and never ever open that door again. But why, what are you hiding from? I know.

While I endure confrontation after confrontation.

WORKING FOR LOVE

Growing daily and beginning to find myself. The Molls
who's fun and confident. When Sam got better, you
took me on holiday. We went to France. It was bliss.
It was bliss to start with.

The lot. Oh yes, we had the lot. Lavender fields and
sand-colored farmhouses. Waking up after eleven
hours sleep, with swollen eyes and fuzzy heads.
Guzzling croissants sodden with butter and jam.
Drinking coffee, mahogany-colored with yellow cream
marbelizing when I poured it in. It was good. This was
a dance after we had rested.

We talked, well, not about us, but we talked.

The evenings were cool and I would wrap myself in
a shawl. Then you started to become cool and a
shawl could not help.

But Jack, we were doing so well. I was looking after
you, I was doing my best.

When out of the blue you told me you had to go to
Paris for a meeting in the morning and would not be
back until the next day.

I remained calm.

"How would you feel if I did this to you?"

"Don't be so stupid Molly, you are not running ten
offices."

"Yes, but what if I suddenly told you in the middle
of our holiday that I was going to meet my publisher
in Paris and I'd be gone for twenty-four hours?"

"Oh, your life is so fucking hard, isn't it?"

You left, Jack. My old buddy, my friend, my equal,
you left, slamming the door of our rented farmhouse.
You revved up the car and, shrouded in dust and

caked mud, you drove off to Paris. Leaving me, but this time I'm not going to feel it's my fault. I'm worth more than this. Why are you trying to break me? I want a marriage, I don't want to be alone in this little house, but you know, I'm less lonely alone here now than I sometimes am with you beside me. Because solitude is strength-giving and peaceful. I have never been as lonely as I have been since I married you.

chapter
30

The thought of Daddy and Grace had made me throw up all night. In the morning I telephoned my aunt, Daddy's sister, I took the train from our little village station and she collected me at the next stop.

We sat in her snug yellow kitchen, drinking coffee and eating boudoir biscuits. The coziness of this woman was all-consuming. I wanted to crawl onto her lap and curl myself around her. I longed to weep into her bosom and be protected.

We sat facing each other.

"Lala, Daddy's having an affair."

"How do you know, Molls?"

I told her about the phone call.

"Oh Christ, I hoped you wouldn't find out. I've known for months, I guessed it."

"But Lala, how could he do this to us, how could he betray Mummy like this? They cannot deceive her, it's disgusting."

"You can't stop them."

"I bloody well can. I won't let them lie to Mummy. I can't possibly watch Grace taking over Mummy's house while Daddy plays games with us all. It's vile to think of the friendship that Grace has squeezed out of her."

"Look Molly, your dad needs Grace. He's had a hell of a life and your mum just isn't there for him. Don't deny that."

"Yes, but they've fooled us, they've used us. I won't allow them to do it."

"Molly, be realistic, a lot of men have affairs. Be bloody grateful it's Grace. Just ignore it and whatever happens, for God's sake don't tell your dad you know."

I was flailing against the current. I was destined to drown, I knew that.

That evening Daddy and I had supper in front of the telly as usual. I could not eat. My heart was exploding in my chest. My hands were shaking. I was furious, I was intensely angry. I couldn't look at him without imagining the two of them humping away. My God, my wonderful father was a liar, a cheat, a deceiver, and I loathed him. I thought I felt as agonized as a wife; my man had hurt me badly.

I washed up and he said, "I think I'll go up now Molls."

Not so fast Daddy, not so fast. My heart was pumping, my entire body was alight with a need for confrontation.

"Are you and Mummy going to get a divorce?"

I still had my back to him, sploshing the suds around a wineglass.

"Of course we aren't."

"I think you should."

"What on earth are you talking about? You must be mad."

Oh yes, smooth, turn the blame around to me.

"I heard you on the telephone last night."

"I don't know what you're hinting at Molly."

"Daddy, I heard you on the phone to Grace."

Don't deny me thrice Daddy, don't do this.

"You prying little bitch, you horrible little eavesdropper."

I spun around in total shock and for one moment we locked gazes. I saw a frightened man and he saw a massive threat to his existence.

"Daddy, I didn't mean to, I just went to the stairs because I thought you were calling Mummy."

"Don't give me that shit Molly. You are a troublemaker, you always have been."

"I am not."

I was sobbing, gasping, gulping; he was standing hurling years' worth of pent-up emotions at me.

"You've always been a nosy little bitch, you've always pried into our lives, it's never enough to be

151

normal, is it, Molly? Oh no, go on the hunt for trouble. We're all fed up with you and your failures. We've done so much for you. Well, I'm fed up with it, I'm fed up with you. Get out of my house, I don't have any energy left for little bitches like you."

My teeth started to chatter. I ran down to the cellar, grabbed my suitcase, and fled to my bedroom. I packed.

I had stopped howling and now felt a terrible pain, a great pain, a great pain right across my chest, cutting deep. My teeth were still rattling frantically, uncontrollably, my jaw was trembling and I couldn't stop this reflex. I packed. What I packed was of no consequence, I certainly had no idea.

Daddy had disappeared and the house was totally silent and terribly sad.

I took my case downstairs, climbed into my car, and drove to London. Sometimes you drive down a motorway and having reached the destination don't remember having done it. It's a nasty feeling, a little echo in one's mind says, Did you stop at those lights? When I see a CAN YOU HELP? sign left by the police reporting an accident, I feel guilty because I wonder if I was there and just didn't notice I ran someone over. This was one of those. I could have knocked cyclist after cyclist down and not have remembered. I just drove, not crying, not even wet-eyed.

Every few minutes I would let out an agonized, totally spontaneous wail. It came from very deep inside of me. From a cavern that had been sealed and now the rock had been moved and the noise came

from the very bottom, echoing through the emptiness.

I parked my little Renault in Battersea. In front of
his flat. I pulled out my case and hauled it up the
stairs.

Music was playing from behind the door. I stood,
breathing heavily, trembling as my hand reached up
to the doorbell.

I heard his feet pad down the corridor; the door
swung open.

"Well, well, what have we here?" He laughed.

"Please can I come and stay with you Peter?"

He was wearing a short terry-cloth bathrobe with
his little legs sticking out of the bottom.

"Oh dear, you're clearly in trouble, I suppose you'd
better come in."

It was hardly a euphoric welcome.

I sat down on his sofa and with immense anger I
spewed out the whole story.

Peter listened. I detected a hint of amusement on
his face. I was overwhelmed with my own misery, my
own hurt, and I had no energy to start to decipher
Peter's reaction. After all, he was all I had now, and I
needed to keep him happy, I could not start to question him. At the end of my monologue he put his arm
around me and ruffled my hair.

"My poor darling, my poor little girl. Well, don't
worry, I'm here now. I'll look after you."

"Oh Peter, will you really?"

"Yes, I will."

I hadn't stopped, I hadn't stopped for one second

to work this out. I had plunged into a pool of self-pity without a thought of the pain the adults around me might have been going through. I couldn't deal with the situation alone. I could not face any reality, I would not stop, sit down, and think.

I ran from one cover to another.

Yet both covers were busy covering themselves.

My poor father had fallen in love. For the first time in his life. After all the pain he had endured he had found a total, caring love and I had plunged head-on to destroy it. Threatening the one source of joy he had been given. As for my mother, my sense of outrage was not really for her. We had been locked in combat for so long that I was simply using her betrayal as an excuse.

I was like a mini-cyclone, shooting into people's lives, with no thought of their feelings. Always gravitating toward a man, the men I thought would validate me. I gave myself to them totally, expecting them to make me happy in return, knowing that this divine species could and would give me a voucher validating my existence. As long as I kept them happy, in the only way I knew how, then we'd be all right.

But we were not. I had just opened a door (or had it opened for me?), I had just crossed a threshold, which would lead to the wolf in the bed.

"What big hands you have, Grandmama."

All the better to beat you with, my dear.

Oh yes, I'd found a real daddy now.

chapter
31

We are not swans. I know that, Jack. Swans are
eternally faithful, but then their life expectancy is only
twenty years, which means they are married, partners,
I mean, for about eighteen. Eighteen years Jack—
perhaps we should have been swans. Then you could
have died. I wish you had. Mrs. Swan would never
have had to go through this.

I cannot believe that I did not see it. I turn around
and around like the ballet dancer on the top of my
music box, looking, searching. But like her all I see is
my reflection in the mirror below. That's no good, is
it? It's all very well to have shapely legs and fleshy,
yet taut thighs leading to an area of magic and
mystery. It's fabulous to look beautiful, as I still do,

but it's not enough, is it? It wasn't enough, was it? I stood like her, waiting, empty, waiting to be made whole. Waiting to be a person. I knew you would make me happy, just as you knew I'd look after you. You'd never met a woman like me, had you Jack? I bet you hadn't.

I lured you with a view of sex you'd never seen before. I did things to you no woman had ever done. I gave with such abandon, such overflowing caring. You told me that provincial women were far more selfish, far more repressed. I blew your mind. I had you in the palm of my hand.

"Molly's caught a big fish." That was what Daddy said. He was so pleased. We never bothered to examine the future, we never stopped to take stock of our long-term expectations.

Oh no.

The glory of meeting a man as radiant and successful as you was the ultimate high. I had been trained to believe totally that I needed a powerful man of wealth to validate me and turn me into a person. I needed to marry and then I would be happy. I would exist as a whole with a sturdy man to give me the security I lacked, to fill me with redemption.

I met you Jack, and you were total. You were everything rolled into a tall success story. But there was more to it. I gave myself to you and I felt a gush of warmth, a thin wire of excitement coursed through my veins, buzzing and vibrating like tiny ball bearings shooting through my vital organs and limbs. I imagine

Working for Love

I felt like a scriptwriter when he at last finds the right person to play the part.

And we did love, we did. In the early days we had an enormous power as a couple. We had both found a soul we had been needing. You made me laugh, you had a wonderful raw humor. Your gauche, ungainly way. I loved you for it. I would gaze at you and worship your lack of pretense. So new to me, this man of steel who did not care for culture or seem to mind about social bullshit.

I respected you so much for your self-made ways, you adored me for my outrageous behavior and extravagant habits and we were so happy.

But what was it that filled us with such security and conviction that slipped away so fast? I know you felt an acceptance. For the first time in your life you were sure. A man with such power and wealth who had been terrified of any human he did not have control of.

To see you in your company performing was immensely erotic. It was a turn-on. Whenever I fantasized about you, you would be at work. Behind your huge desk. Running an enormous meeting. Ordering people about. Such confidence. Total dominance. But if you were removed from your kingdom the emperor became a timid fellow. Not the stuff fantasies are made of. You ached for social grace. You yearned to be at ease. I could do it. You could not. I saw no merit in knowing. But it was out of your reach. With me you sensed (perhaps wrongly) that you could grasp a certain know-how. Poor you, poor darling, it meant so much to you. The veins on your temples would rise, as on an old woman's legs. You would develop a slight quaver to your voice, which was just a tiny bit higher than normal. Terror struck. My brilliant self-made lover was not capable of social intercourse, unless it was he who held the wand.

Of course, my treading the thin line, always knowing how far to take it, my ability to make people laugh (I never felt nervous), you loved me for it. At the start. I did not realize then how much it meant to you. I thought you didn't care. I didn't, you see. We took our own merits for granted and yearned for our partner's merits instead.

And you said to me, "Molly, let's invite everyone famous we know to dinner. Let's invite all your lords and pop stars. We'll mix them with my clients, we'll throw in film stars and we'll show them."

But it didn't work. As a child at a tea party filled with food colorings and additives goes too far, throwing the Jell-O and looking at his mother beseeching, "I *am* having a good time, aren't I, Mummy?" you could never really handle life outside your realm. It didn't work. You later lost interest. If you could not control it—you did not want it. While I who had so thrilled you, so filled you with excitement, placing unknown drawing rooms within your reach, I lost my lure. Those attributes we admired in early days, such a part of what made us individuals, became our enemies. When adulation turned to irritation they fitted the double bill.

Once I remember basking in bliss. I had amazed

myself. The first time we had made love it had been good. But *this* was far more.

"Don't you ever have orgasms?" you asked.

"Please don't worry Jack, I don't. I never have, never ever, so don't even think about it, don't try—it just doesn't work. I love sex with you—it doesn't matter if I don't come."

Two days later you took me to your house. It was a mansion. I had not realized the enormity of your wealth. The package was unraveling and the contents were rosy.

You showed me around, timidly apologizing, and you were endearingly humble. You seemed genuinely thrilled that I was so impressed, that I loved your house. We reached your bedroom; it was vast and woody. You gently sat me on the bed and leaned forward to kiss me. The air was reeking of wealth and power and I lay back on the mattress of your really proper four-poster and felt stirrings of passion I had never experienced before. Your masculinity and deep male instincts were firing, you had an aura of triumph.

When you made love to me you took possession, that night. I handed over my documentation of previous ownership. I became yours. You did things to me that made my back arch and my legs taut. You touched parts of my body I had not known existed. Millimeters of my skin became sponges to soak up new sensations that overtook my entire being, and just as I was at a peak I had never come close to climbing before you would stop—completely. Not letting me touch you once. Just talking to me, whispering, "Oh

Molly, I am going to love you and show you such love."

As if you had a timer on my body, you knew exactly when to resume the same slow buildup, the swift, gentle stroking, the extraordinarily light touches that made me wonder if someone had given you a precise ordnance survey map of my body, that I had certainly never been privy to. Oh Jack, you turned the hidden key, you unleashed such a wealth. A wealth of sexuality—up until that night I had never reached those moments of total blackout, those velvet minutes of fuzziness and loss of control, the edge of pure pleasure, the point of total ecstasy, so out of control and allowing it—and you Jack, so in control and skillful. You took me to an eyrie of pleasure, and I loved you for it. You conquered and I was overcome and total. I had always had a fear of orgasm, I had always felt it was a complete powerlessness, a rather embarrassing, shivering abandonment, a loss of control, resembling the twitching and juddering of an epileptic fit. I lost it all and I did not care. I felt I had handed over a very secret, very private part of myself and with it came a new dependence. I had given away such intimacy, such trust, and you had been my guide.

I loved you at that moment as I had never loved, I needed as I had never needed. As you lay back with your head on the pillow your arm around me, and I cuddled into your chest with a force that made me long to crawl inside you, we knew that our lovemaking had conquered us both and that it was setting the pattern. Oh yes Jack, you could control me, you could take me to that peak and always know when to stop, while I arched my back and begged.

My family could sense the change in me.

"Molly's caught a big fish."

I certainly had. A blue whale.

The family were thrilled. At last Molly would be happy. At last Molly has someone to take care of her. A proper man, a grown-up. While you Jack, you envisaged life with this glorious, giving little girl. She who gazed at you with adoration. Who had awoken your most delicate nerve endings. You were successful, you were rich, you were in control, you were a man of direction. We were purring.

You would take care of me and in return I would be a good girl. But Jack, we all forgot one thing. Even Shirley Temple grew up. They bound her breasts with bandages, but still she grew. As did I. And I grew and grew.

The constant cutting, the repression, the conscious and subconscious battle to keep me subservient, it didn't work. As pruning a rose serves to help it grow, the attacks ultimately gave me remarkable new shoots and I became stronger and betrayed your view of me. And you didn't like this change, did you Jack?

Suddenly I could be confronted without crumbling. I could answer back and believe in myself. I had discovered that the thing I feared most in the world wasn't so bad. The thing I had always run away from. And that was myself. I grew to confront, question, and examine myself. I didn't run for cover or diversion. I had spent so many years skimming the surface like a water beetle, darting from one thing to another, a lesser being; I now ceased and was still. I stopped accepting the blame. I also stopped blaming. For the first time in my life I accepted responsibility.

You shook my foundations, you tried every possible trick to get the little girl back again, at times you nearly succeeded, but I am strong.

This will not work either my darling. You have lost. I have lost you. We have lost each other and caused great suffering.

Is she compliant Jack? Does she do those things I used to do? How are her marketing techniques?

Oh Jack, my heart is smashed, broken open, and causing me so much pain.

chapter
32

Peter told me many things. He told me that my father and Grace were weak people who had used me and Mummy. He filled my mind with strong, dominating words.

"Your father is a selfish, self-opinionated bastard. He's done you no favors. You don't need him anymore, now you have me."

He forbade me to see him and insisted I keep away from home. Daddy telephoned ceaselessly those first few weeks and as Peter had banned any communication, I refused to speak to him. He then wrote a loving, pleading letter and Peter scoffed.

"Don't be his puppet Molly, he's done a fantastic destruction job on you so far. Look at you, yes, look at you, you're a nothing, a nobody, his pawn. You need me Molly, I can teach you, I can turn you into something."

Mummy came back to England and telephoned me.

"But why Molly, why won't you come and see us?"

"I can't tell you that Mummy. But please, leave me alone, Peter and I are doing very well, just let me get on with my life."

And so they did.

Peter was a very bitter man. He was racked with jealousy and envy. He was also a drinker; not all the time, but sometimes, and after countless glasses of Scotch his eyes would start to narrow and the taunting would begin. I could tell it was going to happen. His lips would start to sneer, his voice would develop a singsong quality, and venom would pour out. Accusations, twisted statements, vehement insisting that I had committed some wrong. I would argue, I would plead my innocence. Then he would become violent. Clever violence, physical abuse that could never be detected. He would pin me against the wall and repeatedly bang my head against it. Or once, as I turned to run, he kicked me to the ground and slammed his fists, eight, nine, ten times into my kidneys. I would disappear and sob, then he would come to bed, silent and smoldering. In the morning he would be loving, apologetic, and affectionate. However, he always made it clear that I had deserved my beating.

I missed my family so much. I wanted to be with

them, I felt such confusion. My life was being controlled by a man who said I needed him, who claimed
he loved me, but how could he love me when he
caused me such pain? But maybe I deserved the
pain; there is a song or a poem I remember, the final
lines are:

> You're walking the wire
> Of pain and desire
> Looking for love in between.

I was searching and I was sick. Sick of it all, and
homesick—I missed my mummy and my daddy and
my brother and sisters. I had to do it, I was needing, I
was desperate. I was lonely. I took the train to the
country and walked to the house. I was so excited; I
was going home. I was about to feel Mummy's arms
and see Daddy's glorious form. I could touch my life-
long friends, the sofa, the tables, I could eat off the
smiling, familiar plates, I could tell them how horrid
it had been and they'd understand and help me,
they'd sort this one out for me.

My mother looked up from her telephone call as I
came in; she raised an eyebrow and continued talking. I sat down, she hung up.

"Hello Mummy."

"Hello Babe."

"I've come to see you."

"So I gather."

"I've missed you so much Mummy."

"Don't give me that bullshit Molly."

"I'm not, I miss you all so much."

"I'll get Daddy."

She was frozen, her voice was set at one level, she showed no outward emotion at all as she limped out of the room. I was frightened, my foot was tapping. I looked around the walls, my walls. Surely this could not be.

"Hello Molls."

Daddy looked sheepish.

"Hello Daddy."

"Well, what can we do for you?"

"Nothing, I just came to see you."

"But Molly, you told us to keep out of your life," Mummy snapped.

"But I didn't mean it."

"But you said it."

Oh Christ, oh Christ, think fast, this isn't working. I started to cry.

"Listen Molly, you're nearly twenty. You've got to get on with it. You can't come back crying."

"But Mummy, you don't understand."

"What don't I understand Molly?"

I looked at her, I looked at Daddy, I looked around the room. And then I ran, I ran down the lane to the station, I got onto the next train and I ran all the way back to Peter. My mind was swirling, oh yes, Peter was right, I'd tell him, I'd tell him, he'd be so pleased, so pleased he had been right.

Bang, I fell against the door. Before I could get up I was down again, Peter on top of me, grabbing my hair and hammering my head on the floor.

"You fucking bitch, you lousy fucking bitch. You disobeyed me, you ran to Daddy. Well, I was right, wasn't I? He should have done this to you years ago, then perhaps I wouldn't have to be doing it."

I was laughing, looking at him, laughing, I couldn't stop. It drove him mad, he kept shouting, "Shut up, shut up, or I'll shut you up."

Then he stood up and kicked me, he kicked me and kicked me until my laughter turned to screaming.

He was crazed, it was as if he couldn't stop and I started sobbing, gulping, gasping.

"Now let's see what Daddy has to say."

He walked toward the telephone.

"No Peter, no you can't," I gasped.

He dialed.

"Hello, Thomas, it's Peter. I thought you'd like to hear your little girl. Your little darling. I've given her the beating she deserved. You did it mentally old boy, so I've finished the job. Listen, yes, that's right old boy, that's her you hear. Well, I don't want her anymore. You can have her. You were right, she's a pointless little whore. She's alive, but only just, but that's how she's lived her life, isn't it, my friend?"

I don't know how long I lay on the floor. I could not move. The numbness began to wear off and I could feel the most excruciating pain. Every inch of me ached, certain areas were searing with sharp sensations. I was barely able to focus on Peter's actions, he was whistling as he busied himself. I heard him brush his teeth and go to our bedroom. Before he turned off

167

the light he obviously had a thought and went to the front door and opened it, completely ignoring my body curled up on the floor. We lived in a block of mansion flats. As I lay on the carpet I could feel the cold air shoot up the stairs and over my body.

Then I heard the echo of leather soles on the linoleum. Swiftly darting up the stairs. The draft swept over me as she came in.

"It's all right Molls, you're okay, I'm taking you away now."

I looked up and saw Grace. My Grace, my saving Grace.

She helped me struggle up; I was still in my coat. I gazed at her, unable to comprehend the acceptance in her voice. She put her arms around me and helped me down the stairs. She did not stop for one second, not to gather my belongings or seek out Peter. She simply scooped me up and supported me. As I slowly and agonizingly slipped into her car, Peter threw open the doors of the French windows on our balcony.

"I was doing her a favor," he shouted. "She wants to be dead, don't you realize that, she thrives on pain, she can only survive with rejection and drama."

How my baby survived will always remain a mystery to me. She was conceived in desperation, carried with ceaseless struggle, and yet she survived. We have strong genes.

I hadn't told Peter I was pregnant; I had planned to tell him that night, after I had told Mummy and Daddy, but it had all misfired. My plot had failed. I thought they would all be thrilled. While I, I would have someone to love and I would be loved. I could nurture and care for this baby and it would love me and give me a reason for being.

If I no longer had a family or a daddy, I would provide myself with a new love object. And pregnant women are cared for and cosseted. It seemed simple. I hadn't reckoned on ending up with my entire being battered and homeless.

chapter
33

My younger sister often goes to the supermarket. She
does not go as you or I do, for her groceries, she goes
for physical contact. Believe me, it's true. She often
says, "Honestly Molly, I felt so empty, so unloved, so
I went to the supermarket. I stood looking at the
biscuits and along came a lovely woman who needed
to reach the packets I was in front of, so she stretched
out her arm and said 'excuse me.' I didn't move, so
she brushed my arm, it was lovely. I pretended she
was my mummy, shopping for my supper. Then I
bumped into a man who was studying the frozen
dinners. I said sorry but we touched. You can spend
hours like that, constantly touching, constantly

communicating and watching, seeing what they buy. I crave that closeness Molly."

I understand it, don't you Jack? No you probably don't. You never needed that closeness. You never liked that longing in me, that empty hole craving attention. Neither did Daddy.

I used to long for you to approve of me Jack. For you to come home and listen to me. But you didn't want to.

Neither did Daddy.

Poor old Mummy. I should have learned my lesson, shouldn't I? Perhaps I didn't want to. Perhaps she didn't want to. We were all so busy dancing to our own tunes. Feeling for ourselves, thinking we were being hurt the most. You said at the beginning, the beginning of the end, when you took me out to dinner to tell me you were leaving, "This isn't an eating competition Molly."

But it was a competition, it's all been a competition. Vying for love, vying for attention, never winning. But I never could. You can't compete with people who are dead. And I worked so hard at it. I should have paid more attention. The need for constant reassurance, the need for control, the accusations.

"I'm not your first wife Jack. I'm not a neurotic who will lie and cheat on you. I'm not going to leave you."

"Don't talk about Sarah like that Molly."

"She was ruined Jack, you know it."

"No she wasn't, she was just unpredictable."

"I'm not her and I'm not going to be her, or behave like she did—so stop trying to control me."

Tessa Dahl

Were you frightened Jack? Why didn't I realize?

I had spent my childhood trying to live up to someone who was dead. An angel. I just fell into your trap Jack. I was ripe, wasn't I? I've spent seven and a half years competing with a devil. Your devil, your first wife, the devil in your soul. The devil we never mention. Poor, poor Sarah, did you hurt her like you hurt me or did you become as you are as a result? I promised you Jack, I know I did; I've broken that promise and I'm sorry. It's all right, you can close that door now, you can lock it. I didn't mean to hurt you. I just wanted to open it a crack. But Jack, sometimes we have to allow the pain to surge through us so we can learn.

I remember, I remember an old woman I met years ago, in Hampstead. She was wise and wiry and I wanted to feed off her worn sense, and sensibility; I felt she had a magic. She said to me as I left, "Remember Molly, anyone who makes you work for their love is not worthy of it."

chapter
34

My mother was horrified to be the parent of an unmarried pregnant teenager. Her working-class American roots started to emerge from the ground. They had been covered for years and were now coming up for air. She fought for me to have an abortion but I would not. My father seemed rather pleased that I was pregnant. He supported me totally and we began to build a new and rather exciting relationship.

Grace was somewhere in the middle. She became the most realistic—I don't know how I would have survived without her support.

But what confusion. An appalling mess. Here I was,

carrying the unborn child of a man we all hated. Each of us relating to the pregnancy so differently.

I literally saw it as my salvation. The answer. I centered my entire existence around this little, unknown fetus. I nurtured and cared for myself. I was immersed in the entire process, I placed all my hope, expectation, and unfulfilled love in the swelling of my belly.

My mother showed no interest at all. She would not discuss any aspect of the pregnancy. In fact, she became rather callous. She seemed to want to make me ache. She would look at me with a glint of disdain. She would delight in telling macabre stories of her friends' miscarriages in disgusting detail. She would question my every move and put me down. I remember her turning to me one morning and saying, "I've decided to go away and see my friend Clare. As you're such a great little homemaker, as you look after your father so splendidly, I think you can run the house."

She left. I was eight months pregnant and Daddy was ill. My brother and sisters were at home and I became completely drained. It was her mistake because it drew Grace, Daddy, and me into solidarity. Grace became my friend. She helped me so much during that time. I think she was frightened. I think they both were. I had become very powerful. I was harboring their secret. Of course they played up to it and I played along.

Grace had eased away from her friendship with Mummy. That had been my one request. After the night, the ghastly, unforgettable night that Peter had mashed me to a pulp, I had stayed with Grace for a few days. She nursed me.

During that time we had a major discussion about her and Daddy. It was deeply confusing, it always will be. There was a whirlpool that we were all caught up in and we all needed each other.

Grace had told me of her love for my father. Her unceasing, unquenchable attachment. Join the club Grace, but you can't have him either, not totally. We were bound together with our love for this beacon. Both of us aspiring, longing for the unreachable. He was out of my grasp for a very different reason to hers but we both suffered.

"Your father needs me so badly Molls. He loves your mama, but he has had such pain in his life he deserves some happiness. Your mama can't give him what he needs. I fill him with joy, we love each other, we really do. But Molls, if you want us to end it, if you think we should end it, then we will, but he needs me Molls."

Who was I to tell them to cease? I was part of the drama and the first act hadn't ended yet. Oh no, I was deeply involved and this had thrown me a new life-line to Daddy.

While Daddy, poor Daddy. He was a tired man. A hurting man and he had principles. How could he give up on his poor brain-damaged wife? What could he do to restore sanity to the household?

The lull of happiness that we had all experienced when Grace had first swept in had passed. Mummy,

175

angry Mummy, on reflection I think she was hurting so badly. She centered her fury on my pregnancy, but really it was a mask. In her inner soul she knew her husband was not there anymore. She also suspected my reasons for leaving home and blamed the pregnancy and my return for Daddy's indifference. We were all churning.

I wanted my mummy, but my mummy did not want me. The more she rejected me, the more I turned toward Grace.

Mummy returned from her trip to Clare's. The next morning she faced me in the kitchen.

"Is your father having an affair with Grace?"

"I don't know, Mummy."

"You damn well do know."

"I don't, I really don't."

She gave me one of her long, piercing glares. The type that turned my stomach to acid that sat in my throat.

"Just remember, I'm your mother."

She hobbled off.

As humans we have a deep need to cling on. It is an endearing quality that can be immensely destructive. We stay in relationships way past the point of no return. We stay for many reasons, for security, out of responsibility, for the children, because we are frightened, and because we cannot give up. Sometimes we stay so long past closing time that all the love has been eaten up and spat out. The desperate clawing, the trying to work it out, the memories, the need for partnership, keep us struggling when we should admit it's time to let go. Maybe pride, maybe a thin vein of love, maybe guilt.

Terrible things happen as a result. What could have ended as a happy memory becomes soured and bitter. There is always a reason an affair starts.

The next day she turned to me again.

"They are having an affair. Just tell me Molly, don't deny me, I need you to tell me what I already know."

I couldn't look at her; I felt my entire face flush.

"I don't know, Mummy."

"You do."

"I don't."

"Look at me Molly, look at me, don't do this to me. Look into my eyes and swear they aren't having an affair."

My eyes were filling with hot tears. My baby was moving angrily in my stomach.

"He can't even screw me anymore Molly. He's hurting me. I'm in such pain, I need him so badly."

"Is that all, Mummy? Is that all? Is it just what you need, Mummy? What about what Daddy needs? Am I just your little informant? Am I simply your mole, rooting around? Where have you been, where have you been when I needed you?

"Oh yes, you need me now. Just like Daddy, he needs me now too. We all need so badly, don't we Mummy? That's all our problem, we've all been needing for so long. Like a bunch of baby birds in a nest, with our beaks constantly open, always squawking, pushing the others aside. We are like one, one enormous cuckoo that is always hungry. You, Daddy, and me. Three people existing off each other. Thriving on the pain and drama. I'm your daughter, you bitch. Where am I? Where's my childhood gone?"

"I couldn't help being ill, I couldn't help having my strokes."

"None of us could help this disgusting sorrow we've gone through. It's no one's fault, we've suffered, but Mummy, we're clinging on to the suffering like a Russian Vine. We are all allowing it to continue, blaming each other, never stopping to actually talk, to see how the other people are feeling. We've never learned to tread water, we've just allowed the current to carry us all. Searching for answers, searching for something to fill the void, Mummy.

"I am searching, and I'm so tired of trying to be what I'm not. Of desperately trying to keep you all happy, of searching for fulfillment in all the wrong ways. I've spent so long trying to make up for what I'm not, apologizing for who I am. I feel so worthless Mummy. I know I'm worthless. And now you're becoming worthless Mummy, get out before it's horrid, really horrid. I'm addicted, you're addicted, he's addicted, and no one knows how to stop. It hurts, it hurts so good, doesn't it Mummy, and we've learned to thrive on the pain."

I was amazed, stunned, breathless. Where had all that come from? That outpouring of consciousness, I had never known it was festering inside me. It was out. I sat down and she stared at me, she gazed, transfixed.

She left that night. It was horrible. It was the most

anguished day of my life. She spoke to Daddy only once, it was a snarl, a vicious whisper loaded with hatred.

"I'm going. I'm leaving. I will never, ever come back. Just remember one thing baby, you loved me, oh Jesus, you loved me once."

My sister Meriel carried her cases down the stairs. The stairs that had played such a part in our lives. Meriel could not stop crying. Meriel, who never hurt anyone. Meriel, who had made everyone laugh over the years: Meriel was surrounded by a blanket of sadness. Mathew just stood around looking embarrassed; we'll never know what Mathew feels. He never lets anyone in. Fanny was away, thank God. Daddy had appeared to say good-bye. It was so extraordinary that within twelve hours, twenty-five years of power was ending.

The chance for discussion was gone, there was no skin left to heal, the time for living and loving had long since been eaten up. The music had stopped and everyone was going home.

She sat beside me in the car in silence. We had nothing left to say. As I kissed her at Passport Control she looked at me with a surge of newfound strength.

"You're right Molly, I'm wasting away. I'm going to try to learn how to love life again. I'm going to try to find me. But I want you to remember two things Molly. The first is that we love you, Papa and I, we do love you, we may have done wrong things, we may not have always been there, but we loved you. The second is hard. I want you to love yourself Molly.

Until you love yourself you'll be flailing around forever. Having a baby, trying to please Papa, wanting
everyone to love you, being everyone's Mummy,
searching for love affairs—that is not the answer.
We've never let you really feel you were worth loving, I know that now. There were too many distrac-
tions, too much pain to concentrate on and you always seemed so fine, so resilient, so compliant. And
Molly, thank you, I'm going away to learn to love
myself; it's not too late. I'm hurting, I'm hurting so
much, but it has to get better."

We clung to each other for what seemed like minutes but was surely seconds. I was weeping, she was
weeping. I felt as if my entire being had been swept
away.

We went to bed that night with such grief. We were
all mourning, we were stunned, we were completely
lost. At three A.M. I jumped up and rushed to the
bathroom. Liquid was gushing from between my
legs, I had become totally incontinent, it wasn't until
I sat down on the lavatory that I realized my waters
had broken.

Daddy and I drove to the hospital; there was nothing left to say. Our emotions were spent, we were in
shock.

He did not stay and I did not want him to. We both
had important jobs to do and had to get on and do
them. I knew he needed to be with Grace. I knew I
needed to have the baby, I had no choice. He stayed
and made sure I was safe and comfortable.

"I'm off now Molls, I think you'd better get on with it. I'll call you in a few hours."

"All right Daddy." I attempted a smile but I was overcome by a powerful contraction.

Then he turned to me and with such inner struggle he kissed my forehead.

"I love you Molly."

I didn't call for any of them. I screamed, I shouted, I lost control—nothing could have prepared me for the pain. As Daisy's head stretched and split my being, the world was on fire, I was consumed with searing, scorching. My core was a fireball.

Yet I didn't beseech or beg for any of them. Not Mummy, not Daddy, not Peter.

At that moment of heightened awareness, my subconscious knew, I was on my own.

chapter
35

We don't learn without the lessons. We can't grow
without the pruning and it takes a lot of very hard
work to break our childhood patterns.

I have spent seven and a half vital learning years
with you Jack. I know now what I did not know then.
I thank you for it.

I thank you for marrying me and loving both Daisy
and me. I apologize for casting you as I did. But Jack,
you were so perfect and you played the part
beautifully. The "emotionally unavailable man" with
whom I struggled for each childhood longing. I did
love you, though, I really did, I loved you in a way
that was so devoted, so needy, and so dependent.

When Daddy married Grace I was pleased for

them, but where did that leave me? They were in love, totally and unconditionally. They had traveled a long way and they deserved peace and happiness. Suddenly I was redundant; it was healthy but I was not.

Mummy knew I was suffering a terrific sense of loss. She was living in America and had really rediscovered her self-confidence and strength. Daisy and I went to spend the summer with her. Our future was a mist of uncertainties. Grace was now the mistress of the house, Daddy belonged to her—I knew I couldn't stay at home. I remember the night I met you Jack. You were there on holiday. I remember lying in bed and thinking, this is what I want, this is what I need, I've found what I've been searching for. I can love this man, this poor soul. He needs me, he looks so sad. How could his wife have killed herself, how could she, he seems such a lovely, caring man?

Mummy said how much you reminded her of Daddy.

We've gone full circle Jack. We must never forget the extraordinary movements, the cherishing, the immense power our love had. We must never discredit our seven and a half years.

It is agony to let go of an obsession. To wave good-bye to one's major motivation. To start living for oneself and not try to earn love and approval. I knew that we could destroy each other ultimately; you knew that. That is why, I suppose, in retrospect, you left. I would have gone on; perhaps we should have tried. But it wouldn't have worked. I wonder if marriage should be on a seven-year guarantee. Every seven years we could examine the pros and cons and renew the contract if mutually desirable.

I have found a stillness. I have found a peace.

As I said at the beginning, I blame no one, we all danced with each other, some of us have changed partners, some of us are alone. But we all grew and we all loved.

I remember so much. I feel such genuine gratitude. But I'm frightened. You have that little Barbie doll, sweet Patsy, that little office manager. I knew really, I've known for a long time.

I have no one.

I have no one to follow. As I once followed you Jack. I'll tell you a secret. It's no big deal, but it always made me uneasy when I thought of it. My version of infidelity, and so early on.

We had been married for three days. Daddy drove us to the airport. We were leaving to live in Manchester, well, Prestbury, Cheshire. I had a very heavy heart that day. You were so sparky, you were filled with confidence, barking orders at me about luggage and tickets. Like a lamb to the slaughter. We stopped at the barrier. You tapped your foot with irritation, you wanted to get going.

I turned to Daddy, I looked into his eyes, they were suspiciously emotional. Oh no Daddy, don't cry! Don't do this now, not now. I turned to you Jack, and your face was displaying total impatience and irritation. "Come on Molly, let's get moving."

"Good-bye Daddy."

"Good-bye Molls."

I hugged him, I hugged him so hard. I gave him twenty-three years' worth of unsung adoration. I looked at him and for an agonizing moment I didn't know who to go with. I looked at you Jack, and then at him and my confusion was indescribable.

"You'd better go Molls."

"Yup, I know."

I watched him turn and walk away from me. That giant of a man, my love, my life, I stood still and yearned. I watched him stooped and limping, wind his way through the crowd, I watched until he disappeared.

"For Christ's sake Molly, let's get this show on the road."

I followed you Jack. My eyes were filling with tears.

"Molly, grow up."

And I did, eventually. And you didn't like it, did you Jack?

But I do.

I really do.